I0571259

NAKED
I CAME

NAKED
I CAME

IAN KUMAR

Text Copyright @ by Ian Kumar

TXu 1-947-940

All rights reserved.

This is the work of fiction. Any resemblance of characters to actual persons, living or dead is purely coincidental. The Author holds exclusive rights to this work. Unauthorised duplication is prohibited. No part of this book can be reproduced in any form or by electronic or mechanical means including information storage and retrieval systems, without the permission in writing from author. The only exception is by a reviewer who may quote short excerpts in a review.

ISBN 978-0-9969059-0-9

Editors: Seema Lall and Mahima Singh

Formatting: Damonza

To those who fall on the way-side,
a prey to their vices/carnality…

…And to a son who missed his father

TABLE OF CONTENTS

ACKNOWLEDGEMENTS

Thanks to family and friends for their invaluable input
&
to Mahima my daughter for her valuable assistance

PROLOGUE

NAKED I CAME is the story of Justin, a young man who was transitioning from his adolescence years to adulthood and beyond. Growing in age and experience, he experiments as any normal person would, when sexual awareness unfolds before him at various stages of life in the land of India. After completing college education, he secures a much-coveted job in a bank and successfully scales to middle management level in the protocol of the bank. Well settled in life, he feels a nudge from God to join a church as a full-time pastor. Soon he is propelled from an ordinary person into a person who is revered by the congregants of his church.

Life brings him to another turn when after several years in the church, Justin, now a married man, gets involved in an extra-marital affair with one of his congregants.

Principles of Bible come into play...

Justin rejects God and plans to settle in the land of America to start life afresh with his inamorata. God catches him again, and this time, the end-results are beyond Justin's comprehension. The consequences of sin overtake Justin like a tsunami! Separation from his sons torments him constantly.

This is a narration of how ministers of solo churches even solo mega churches risk their entire ministry, life and career when they succumb to temptations and become an easy prey to the lustful desires of the flesh. Alas…Even after repentance, they fall repeatedly.

Is repentance good enough to stop one from sinning further?

What is 'The mystery of three Rs' that leads to the fourth?

Ian Kumar, much influenced by the style of Ernest Hemingway and King James Version of the Bible, has his own peculiar way of bringing alive the narratives. His explicit narration of the facts of life, graphic at times, will bring the reader face-to-face with the realities of life.

This book elicits the happenings that often beset even the most committed leaders at the helm of affairs, who may be at the apex of churches, organisations, institutions, etc. This book is not against 'the system', but it is an attempt to caution 'the resilient yet the ignorant' who may otherwise be trapped in the vices of this world and may end up in oblivion.

ADOLESCENCE

I T WAS A perplexing experience that Justin started under-going from his adolescent years. The bulge now was a permanent fixture, and he could not ever figure out how to wriggle out of that situation. The boys of his age group were still not allowed to wear long pants, white shorts were the permitted outfit in the school with tucked-in half-sleeve shirt, a belt with green and yellow stripes and a matching tie.

The sixties in India were quite an orthodox time. Justin's parents never contemplated having a discussion on sex education neither with him nor with his younger sister. One had to gather—or stumble upon—the information by oneself. Imagine *no* books on the subject of sex education, *no* internet, and *no* computer. Compared to the 21st century, those were like medieval times.

Unfortunately, to counter his battle of the bulge and to take charge of the unruly head so that it be kept under submission, there were no Jockeys or Hanes tailor-made underpants available at that point in time. The underpants worn were hand-stitched by moms at home. It crossed Justin's mind several times to use a ban-dage and tie the barging pole to the more 'acceptable' muscle of the lower part of the body: the upper thigh. However, some sane thought never let him take that action, and today, he shudders to imagine the consequences of his adolescent mind's 'remedy' to the problem.

Ultimately, Justin grew out of the ignorance, and while stepping into the teen years, he researched extensively on the subject and earned a self-proclaimed doctorate in it before he exited that phase of life. His research brought to his understanding the fact that, in the remotest likelihood of a pole vault event taking place, his own equipment or 'the pole' could be used, but unlike the regular bamboo pole—which is discarded at the height of the obstacle—this 'pole' needed to be carried along after the hurdle was crossed—*obvious!* By his mid-teens, Mama's home-stitched under pants were out and some V-shaped, elasticised cotton underpants, which could be bought in the market, were available to deal with the ever-bulging situation. The other self-made remedial measure was to carry a book, which could be held in front and over the troublesome area that would otherwise attract a range of disapproving to disgusting looks from the elders, disdain from boys, and spasmodic laughter from girls in the school. Holding the book in front would totally change the equation by giving the impression of a very likable, decent, and a studious young man with a somewhat humble and confused expression.

The X-chromosome was a better species wherein, after a while, they would come to terms with their protruding assets. Remember, in those days, the salwar suit for girls always had a third piece called *chunni* (stole), which—if thrown over the shoulders—afforded a decent covering. How Justin wished the Bollywood superstars of those eras, Rajesh Khanna or Baba Jitender, had started such a trend for men where boys could carry a stole, which, in times of need, could be used to cloak their wares. Well! It was not to be so.

JAIPUR

ANAGING THE PROBLEMS of his teen years and being on the threshold of adulthood, Justin graduated from high school and started hunting around for a college. Though not too brilliant in mathematics, majoring in science was his dream. However, the probability of getting into a science college of Delhi was very tough and Justin did not stand a chance. In light of the situation, it was decided that Justin should seek admission in one of the colleges in the city of Jaipur in Rajasthan, where a slightly lower percentage may be acceptable. Arrangements were accordingly made for him to stay with the family of one of their relatives, Mr. and Mrs. David, who were living in that city.

The family of the elderly Mr. and Mrs. David, with three boys and two girls, was simple and unassuming. The three boys slightly older than Justin were still struggling to get through the high school, whereas the two girls in their mid-twenties were pursuing a professional course. The older one, named Poonam, was the younger sister of Mrs. David and the younger girl, named Shelly, was the daughter of Mr. and Mrs. David. Fair maidens with long hair, both had petite structures.

Talking endlessly, listening to popular Bollywood songs and feasting on home-cooked mutton curry were the passions indulged into by the family, the order of activity being interchangeable. Earning livelihood was the prime responsibility of the womenfolk. Mr. David, who had taken up early retirement from the job that otherwise also could never sustain the whole family, had his own preference of listening to the world news on the family-owned transistor radio. The verbal bout between the family members over the radio during primetime was always spectacular to listen to for an outsider. It seemed special care was taken to clear the vocal chords of every member of the heptagon family by the midwife during their respective births. Bickering, arguments and cohesiveness—forces otherwise diverse in nature—worked hand-in-hand in this family. They fought for the same things and came together over those very things.

The three-floor family house on the main road could be easily identified from the rows of other houses by the very beautiful, tall and big-but-lean German shepherd that took pleasure in stationing itself on the top of the third floor terrace parapet wall. Called 'Tiger', the German shepherd was the common love of the heptagon. His fawn and white-coloured fur coat with big, beautiful expressive eyes made Tiger a darling of everyone. As is famous for this breed being a one-man dog, Tiger was most faithful to the middle son, Rishi. Every day in the morning, Rishi used to take Tiger for a walk when passersby would throw appreciative glance at the beautiful four-legged creature that moved majestically with its head held high. Rishi carried a ball and Tiger would walk beside him, looking expectantly for the ball to fly out of his hands so that he could race behind and intercept it midway—holding the ball in his big mouth as a prized catch—and walk back triumphantly.

Justin soon became a part of the family and was always treated with more respect than was commanded by the three brothers combined. All assignments that needed extra care and dependability came his way. One of the daily tasks of importance for the family was the commute of the two young women to their vocational college. This needed dependability, punctuality, skill and equipment. The main mode of individual transportation in the bustling city was the bicycle. Justin was the proud owner of a dark green Sunbeam bicycle, fitted with two side-view mirrors and sports handlebar that gave one the feel of riding a motorcycle.

The two girls ready in their starched chiffon saris were always on the lookout for a more reliable, expert, and fast ride to drop them to their training institute. Justin excelled in all these areas and there were always undercurrents between the two maidens as to who could ride on the rear carrier seat of his bicycle.

Endowed with a sharp-witted tongue, Poonam was the fairer of the two. In the morning, she would somehow always manage to position herself next to Justin's bicycle and thus lay her claim over a ride with him. Shelly, the younger one, on the other hand, would usually be left behind to take the ride with one of her brothers on their old bicycles, which were usually dirty and had less-inflated tires. Plus, there was always the ever-present risk of the ride being abandoned midway because of some inevitable and nearly routine malfunction in the bicycle, thus necessitating a bail out that would not be available to the damsel in distress. Whenever Shelly got pushed to take a ride with one of her brothers, missing her chance to make a safe bet by riding with Justin, he could perceive sorrow on her face.

This early morning squabble was a daily affair and everyday Justin confronted two pair of eyes; one gleaming victoriously and the other with a sea of sadness in them. Sadness is always more profound than happiness and it started to touch Justin more with each passing day. As a result, he started playing small tricks each morning, by running back to the room on the third floor to fetch another book or his fountain pen, that were supposedly left behind, so that by the time he would come down, Poonam, who would be fuming by then, would leave in a huff with one of the brothers. Shelly saw the efforts Justin made to side with her, and in return, she started taking special care of his needs. She would pour out a select portion of curry for him, specially cook fresh *chapattis* for him, take care of his laundry and be more observant about his daily needs.

COLLEGE

THE 'BOYS ONLY' college was uneventful except for the fact that the whole college community was vertically divided in three sects. Two sects belonged to different regional groups, with their never-ending disputes mostly being settled with swords and *lathis* (bamboo sticks). The third group, which did not have any regional bearings, was the one that suited Justin. Built on a sprawling campus, the college had big playing fields all around. However, the main activity for the students on those playing fields was the training given by the National Cadet Corps known as 'NCC'. The NCC imparted two training courses for the students—the infantry division and the armored division—and Justin joined the latter. War with China in 1962 and then with Pakistan in 1965 had greatly aroused patriotic feelings in Justin; plus, he always wanted to join the 'Indian Air Force' to become a fighter pilot.

Sand dunes on the outskirts surrounded the city of Jaipur in Rajasthan. Many a times, during the summers, the evening sky would suddenly turn red and sandstorms would lash the city.

Justin took college very seriously and did better in his first year than what he had ever accomplished in his entire history in school. Many a times, when there was no class for a long stretch, he would quickly cycle down to the house and sit to study. Everyone in the heptagon family was impressed with the serious attitude Justin had towards his studies because they themselves lacked it completely.

Shelly, who by now had completed her apprenticeship training and had joined the firm as a full-time receptionist, was usually home by the time Justin came back from college. After a busy day, Justin liked to relax a bit, and talking with Shelly was his way of relaxation. They would just talk about the food cooked for the evening or current movies or Shelly would share about her day at work. They would sit down and just enjoy the time they spent together. On one such occasion, Justin noticed Shelly glancing repeatedly in his direction in a way that made him squirm, feel awkward, and in fact, he sort of felt as if he was naked. Being his senior by at least 4 to 5 years, Shelly never had any reservations while talking to or dealing with Justin. In the days to come, this game picked up in momentum. Whenever the two of them were alone, Justin would feel Shelly's piercing eyes scanning the area of the seams of his pants, so much so that his right hand would repeatedly reach the zipper of his pants to ensure it was fastened properly.

In the beginning, Justin had no illusions because it was customary in India to give every relationship a decent name. If the girl was older, even by a few years, it was customary to call her *Didi*, and if the boy was older, one was supposed to call him *Bhaiya*. Anyone much older was patented as Aunty or Uncle. The culture of calling someone boyfriend or girlfriend was simply not prevalent. Every relationship outside the blood relation started this way, and anything outside this periphery of defined kinship that was carried on the sly culminated in an unacceptable alliance with stigma attached to it by the society. In that part of India, during the late sixties, there did not exist any relations termed 'friends'. At Justin's age, friends were the people who studied together in the same class and were supposed to be people of same gender; mixing freely with the other gender was not the norm of the day.

The 'illusion' ultimately started to dissipate and things slowly started becoming more evident. The gaze was rather obvious; it gave Justin a very strange feeling of excitement. However, he could never gather courage to talk openly with Shelly.

College studies were progressing at a brisk pace and Justin kept up with them as a routine. One evening after a long day at college, Justin returned home and stretched out on the carpet in the living room. On that hot summer evening, everyone else was having the late afternoon siesta. Shelly had just come back from work and went straight into the kitchen to prepare the evening meal for the family. Justin, resting on his side with his right arm supporting his head as a pillow dozed off but his mind was awake, as he could still make out every squeak that emanated from the ceiling fan. With eyes closed, he was still able to perceive the brightness of the hazy sun that permeated the room through the nearby window, when he felt a shadow falling across. Lazily, he opened his eyes to find Shelly standing next to him. They exchanged half-smiles and Shelly sat down on the carpet next to him, too close for comfort. Justin felt adrenaline run through his veins but quickly closed his eyes to clear his mind of any deplorable thoughts.

After a few minutes, he slowly opened his eyes and found Shelly also lying down on the carpet facing him. She was wiping off the perspiration from her face with her *chunni*.

'Tired?' he asked.

'Yes, it was very hot in the kitchen', she said, softly dabbing her face all the while.

With the *chunni*[1] doing the job of a handkerchief and not what it was supposed to do, her chest was left open to the gaze of Justin. He could see her bra clearly outlined through the upper shirt, which had become damp by her sweat. As if that was not enough of a temptation for Justin, Shelly unwittingly propped up

---

1 Stole

herself on her arm, which made her breasts push forward, exposing the well-formed mounds and the deep valley in-between. Small beads of sweat trickled down from the mound into the valley and from there onto the other mound. Justin quickly took his eyes off the sight as if caught stealing, but Shelly, with her eyes closed, was unmindful of it. Sleep was now miles away from his eyes. With her eyes closed, it became difficult for Justin to understand if Shelly had dozed off or was just resting.

Justin had a strong desire to, once again, look at Shelly but … his conscience was pricking him. The tug between desire and conscience was at its peak when Shelly's hand lightly touched his fingers. Justin slowly opened his eyes and observed that Shelly with her eyes still closed was breathing heavily. Every time she inhaled, her breasts pushed forward a little more, the sight of which increased Justin's palpitation. He felt a lump in his throat, his whole body started to shiver, and his mind started to conjure up wild images that were not proper for him to entertain. He was scared to do what he should not do, but was tempted to play Adam. At last, against his better judgment and taking care not to disturb Shelly, he very slowly and gently started closing the gap between his fingers and her cleavage. While travelling the distance near her face, his hand could feel the warmth of her breath. He hesitated for a moment, but then gathering courage that he never possessed before, he very slowly kept up the journey of his hand towards the most desirable assets of Shelly.

The moment he cautiously slipped his fingers under her clothes, he felt the heat that had the potential of scorching the lines on the palm of his hand and change his fate forever. Very slowly, he rested the tips of his left hand fingers, on the skin of her breasts, which were moist with the sweat. She stirred slightly and her clothes made way to a deeper glance of appreciation for Justin. Her areola—the brown skin around her nipples—was now partially exposed. While her hot breath was fanning the skin of the back of his hand, the insides of his palm was feeling the heat that radiated from her body. Then, as if by an unknown force, he let his hand slide furthermore and very lightly cupped the moist-warm flesh of her breasts. Without so much as a warning, Shelly opened her eyes and, with her right hand, held Justin by the wrist. 'Dead' was the first thought that came to his mind. He had never felt so ashamed in his entire life. The flow of adrenaline was now suddenly replaced by a spasm of fear. Words of apology poured out by themselves, genuinely supplemented by the sorrowful expression that now covered his face. He tried to set his shaky hand free from her gentle grip, but Shelly, looking straight into his eyes, held onto it. Shame coupled with panic had overtaken Justin. Oh man! Is she going to call others to witness the horrendous act committed by him in his lustful innocence?

Lust and innocence do not go together, but that is exactly what happened. Apart from a stolen kiss here and there, followed by an exchange of puppy love notes during his school time, his innocence was never under attack with such deadly mix of lust. He again tried to express his sincere regret, when she shushed him with her finger and patted his head back onto his arm, the make-shift pillow. His left hand was still in her grip, of course now outside her clothing. He was still trembling within himself. Whether it was out of excitement of trespassing the unknown territory or fear of treading the wrong path, Justin could not understand! He was all shaken up, but he could not make out the true feelings of Shelly about the whole thing.

ADULT PATHWAYS

ECOND SEMESTER OF the year was ending, and the exams were approaching faster than desired. Justin started burning more of the proverbial midnight oil, in order to do well in his exams. He would set up his alarm clock for the wee hours of the morning, with the thermos flask full of hot tea at his bedside to give him a jumpstart. He would deliberately keep his alarm clock at a distance from his bed, so that he may not have easy access to it. As the alarm sounded at the appointed hour, he always had to jump out of bed to turn it off, lest the sound would disturb others at those unearthly hours.

Along with being regular in his studies, he always practiced faith in God that was deeply ingrained in him by his mother—a petite woman by stature, but strong in faith. She ensured that Justin and his younger sister always went to Sunday school in their pre-teen years. Thereafter, in their teen years, their mother accompanied them to Sunday services at a nearby Baptist church. The three of them attended most of the evangelical conventions held there. He remembered the time when a preacher in one of the conventions exhorted the assembly for giving towards some good cause and Justin took off his wristwatch and put it as offering in the collection bag. At other times, very often, he used to respond to the altar calls by raising his hands or going forward for prayer. However, in Jaipur, while living with the David family, he missed all that, as these people were not regular churchgoers.

As the exams approached, Justin started to fast and pray. However, the soaring temperatures and long summer days did not make it an easy task. While observing a fast on such days, he would go up on the terrace in the evening and impatiently look at the setting sun. As soon as it had set, he would run down to break his fast and satiate the pangs of hunger.

Shelly knew the importance of examination time for Justin, and she made sure that he gets a peaceful atmosphere for his studies, going to the extent of enforcing a curfew on anyone and everyone at home in order to keep the volume of transistor radio low. At last, the exams were over and Justin fared well in them. The whole family was relieved as the restriction so arbitrarily enforced by Shelly as regards to the radio had ceased.

After the exams were over, everyone at David family decided to spend an evening out to watch a movie and have fun, as by the end of the week, Justin needed to go back to Delhi to spend time with his parents during the summer vacations.

Dressed up in their casuals with the girls paring up with the boys on their bicycles, they started their journey in the cool of the evening. Of course, as always, Shelly was sitting behind Justin on his bicycle. The moment they hit the road they started racing with each other through the evening rush of the city. These races were fun, weaving their bicycles in and out of the traffic with the girls clutching tightly to the riders, the boys tried to establish their supremacy by cycling down the fastest. Justin was really very good at that and with Shelly sitting on the bicycle behind him, clutching him tightly at the waist, the incentive was enough for Justin to put all his energy to win the mini races. Once at the theater, they had their pick of coke and potato chips and settled in their seats. Poonam always tried to play the spoilt sport on such occasions but somehow Justin and Shelly managed to sit together that night in the theater. Braving the tantrums of Poonam, Justin and Shelly would go to great lengths to ensure that their sitting together would appear normal to the rest of the family. The trio of the brothers was least interested in such squabbles. The movie turned out to be an emotional drama, based on the life of an orphaned boy who at a very young age had to weather all sorts of upheavals in life. Justin and Shelly found themselves crying silently during the movie. Holding each other's hands tightly, they found themselves tossed around by the heart-rending scenes. The nineteen reels footage of the movie became a virtual reality for them, in which they shared similar emotions.

On their way back home, both were silent; Justin did not want to be a part of any bicycle race this time and continued to ride slowly. Driven by the gusty winds, the garbage strewn around on the roadside was furiously rolling past Justin's bicycle as if challenging him to speed up and beat it. Justin who was always on the lookout for such challenges did not pick up this one, allowing the garbage to win by default.

Sitting silently on the rear carrier seat, Shelly lightly rested her head on Justin's back, and held him around his waist. By the time they reached home, everyone else had gone upstairs to their rooms. Justin quietly brought his bicycle to the stand, where a small bulb with an aluminum conical cover hung loosely from the ceiling and dimly lit the area of the stairs that led to the upper rooms. Constantly moved by the wind, which was blowing hard, the bulb struck the wall with its shade repeatedly, producing a strange clanging sound that disturbed the serenity of the atmosphere. Justin put his bicycle on the stand and turned around to see Shelly who by now was sitting on the steps that led to the upper rooms.

'What happened?' asked Justin, when she patted the space next to her gesturing him to sit down. Justin quietly sat down next to Shelly on the steps and softly asked if she was okay. She did not say anything; instead held his hands and laid her head on his shoulder. He slowly put his arm around her shoulders and drew her near him. She looked up to him; her brown eyes, which looked much softer in the dim light, were speaking some strange language that Justin could not understand.

He lifted up her face and softly asked, 'What?'

She did not speak a word, just closed her eyes. Justin looked at her beautiful face and the long neck that was straining towards him; slowly without warning, he found himself bending towards her until his lips lightly rested on hers. For a moment, they stayed like that and then her lips parted to meet his. Suddenly, both became alive to their feelings, their lips pressed hard against each other's, as if both through that kiss wanted to draw on elixir of life from each other. The heat generated between the two had burned the whole atmosphere around them. They remained in each other's arms for a blissfully long period, as 'time' stood still, to absorb the passion of the two lovers... Suddenly, they heard the door creaking and saw Tiger emerge from the upper room. Phew! Justin let go a sigh of relief for it could have been Poonam also. Reluctantly, they got up and started up the flight of steps to their rooms.

Justin could not sleep the whole night; tossing and turning in his bed, he relived the moments repeatedly, until the crack of the dawn brought the chirping of the birds. Now all that had gone to slumber were slowly stretching themselves to welcome the morning sun. The faucet, left open in the night, slowly started to cough up and at the strike of five o'clock, a mixture of air and water started to flow out of the spout; the sound of the sporadic jet of water into the aluminum bucket kept under it served as an alarm for light sleepers to rise. The faint sound of the conch, coming from a distant temple, could be heard. The tinkering of the kettle told that someone was preparing the morning tea. All of a sudden, there was a loud thud indicating that the vendor had just dropped the morning newspaper. Justin, with a half drawn smile on his lips, dreamy eyes, and clutching the soft pillow that gave him a warm feeling, was still not willing to leave his bed.

Slowly, the distinct calmness of the wee hours, started to drown by other sounds of the early morning activities; until, finally, a few minutes later the ever-increasing din of the city life took over the serenity of the approaching dawn.

Coming out of the slumber, while Justin was trying to give a philosophical meaning to the merging sounds of the early morning that ultimately culminate into the fuzzy humdrum of the day, he felt a tap on his shoulder. Shelly was standing there with very soft looks in her eyes and the newspaper in her hand.

'Are you not going to drop me to work today?' she inquired while placing the rolled up newspaper on his bed.

ON A ROLLER COASTER

THINGS STARTED CHANGING very fast in the lives of Justin and Shelly, and they started looking for opportunities to be together. They were always on the lookout for a place where they could steal a kiss or hold each other in their arms. In a house with six more occupants, it was never easy and with the ever-present roving eye of Poonam, it was most of the time a kiss-and-run situation.

With the enemy on the prowl close behind, Justin and Shelly always had to come up with ideas to spend some time together. Their favourite place was the dimly lit staircase where they would hold each other in tight embrace, kissing and stealing each other's warmth. It was the same staircase where Shelly moved her hands under his clothes for the first time and held him intimately. It was the same staircase where one day after taking Justin to new heights of arousal Shelly still had drops of the colourless viscous fluid smeared on her hands, when they were nearly jumped upon by Poonam. It was a close call! One could see the frustrated look on Poonam's face, of having missed an opportunity to catch them. Fuming and cursing under her breath like a tigress that could not pounce upon its prey, she walked away. With each passing day, Shelly and Justin were learning to live more dangerously.

It was no more the desire of the flesh alone that burnt in them, slowly a mature understanding of love started to develop.

Except at the places of profession and career, every other place Justin and Shelly could be seen together. Shelly took upon herself to look after all his needs from taking care of his closet to serving food in his plate. On the other hand, Justin took upon himself all that a man needs to do for his ladylove. They were deeply in love.

Shelly was getting into good age, but in the absence of any good proposals and lack of finances, no one in the family talked seriously about her marriage. In fact, the parents avoided discussing the topic. Things were not easy for the family, as the income never matched the escalating expenses; saving of any type could never be contemplated. Love marriages were not prevalent in those days and Rajasthan never boasted of an ultra-modern society. Christians were mostly depicted in Bollywood movies as a more modern sect, wearing polka dot skirts and western dresses with a glass of wine in their hands, making confession to a priest attired in a white robe wearing a pectoral cross on his person. On a reality check, they were as much a part of the general society and as orthodox as one can be. The only difference being that they did not have any caste system and treated everyone as equals in the true Gandhian spirit. Dowry was not a custom among the Christians, but providing the girl with all the things needed to start a new family was a dream of all parents, and that was a tall order for Shelly's parents.

By now, everyone had come to terms with the idea of Shelly travelling with Justin to her work place. Bicycle for them was not only the mode of transportation but also presented an opportunity where the love-starved duo would find togetherness away from the prying eyes. Justin rearranged his study schedule around Shelly's work schedule, and every day in the evening when she was getting off from work he would be there to pick her up.

She would sit on the rear seat of the bicycle very close to him, to the extent that her breasts would crush against his back. For Justin, the young man in his early twenties, that closeness of Shelly, on an open road, would literally transform his whole back into an erogenous zone releasing the invisible pheromones, which in turn demanded further gratification. To pacify him, Shelly would sneak her right hand around his waist, going through under his jacket until she could reach for *him*. Every day after coming back from their small trip, Shelly would go and wash her handkerchief that had witnessed the climax of the evening. They had become such expert in this art, that on the busy city road no one could ever guess their little secret.

Good times—always fly-by very quickly, and the desire to hold them forever—futile. Justin was about to finish his three-year degree course and so it was decided that before he went back to Delhi, they all should visit Shelly's maternal uncle who lived in Anand, a city in Gujarat. Anand, also called the milk capital of India, posed a peculiar problem to Justin; situated on the Western coast of India, strong winds constantly lashed the city. Being very particular about his hairstyle, Justin had to tie a large handkerchief around his head to keep his hair from being constantly ruffled by the wind. The problem did not mitigate even when once inside the second floor apartment; the abode of Shelly's uncle. To save on electricity, the doors and windows were usually kept open letting the breeze pass right through the living area. Shelly's uncle was a soft-spoken man, as all Gujaratis were. Even the taste of their food had a touch of sweetness.

During the day, they all used to go around the nearby market places and in the evening had fun time in the living area of the apartment. By night, they would roll out their beds on the floor of the big living room and talked the night out. On the last day, Shelly's uncle called Shelly and Justin aside for a talk. The very mention that he wanted to have a word with them in private brought a feeling of tightness to Justin's chest. Did he see them…? Did he eavesdrop on them…? Justin always got scared of such phrases, constantly fearing that someone might get wise to their secret.

'You seem to like each other a lot,' her uncle said in a

meaningful way. Justin skipped a beat; there it goes he thought, in the process losing some colour on his face, while her uncle held their countenance with his steady but strangely enough, a very kind gaze.

'What do you say about Shelly, Justin?' asked her uncle intently looking at them.

Justin made a whining sound. Moving uncomfortably in his seat and trying hard to let not his fear betray his expressions he said, 'Yes, she is a very nice person'.

'Have you ever thought of marriage? Shelly will make a very good wife'.

Yes, yes, yes! Someone has ultimately become wise to their little secret. Justin just wanted to run away somewhere, hide himself, become invisible; surely, this was not happening.

'What do you say?' asked her uncle softly pressing his point of view.

People of age and experience, do have a way of cornering the younger generation and seem to have that uncanny way of looking right through them. Justin slowly answered, 'I don't know Uncle, never thought about it'.

'There is no hurry Justin, I noticed your closeness with each other and wanted to make a suggestion'.

'I understand', was all Justin could say.

The day became uncomfortably long and Justin felt as if everyone was paying them extra attention. He felt utterly exposed by their unpresumptuous side-glances.

Back in Jaipur, Justin and Shelly needed to face their relationship in the light of the perspective given to it by Shelly's uncle. They started talking on the subject but Justin had his own fears about marriage and thereafter. Until now because of the age difference he had always given respect to Shelly, he wondered how they would reverse the situation after marriage. Shelly tried to reassure him by saying that things will change and she will give him the respect a husband deserves, in fact would always address him respectfully.

Well, what about the age difference...? People often say that girls mature quickly after childbirth. Justin had always envisioned a wife who will remain fair and lovely forever. It was not just a physical relationship between Justin and Shelly; they really loved each other's body, mind and soul. However, Justin had a strong feeling that after a few years of marriage Shelly would age faster, and though their love was not shallow, yet the age factor was bound to make a difference in his feelings towards her and he did not want to hurt her.

Dealing with the complexity that they now faced about their future but reaching no conclusion, it was time for Justin to go back to Delhi as his graduation had completed.

ADIOS

ELHI, THE METROPOLIS, was a bustling city, and Justin became very busy in the process of job hunting. He missed Shelly a lot. The only way of communication between them was by the way of postal mail, and that took at least five to six days to cross the boundaries between the states before the postman could deliver the love letters laced with the perfumes of his sweetheart. Justin's family could not afford the luxury of a telephone, which was a rare commodity, with more often than not the ornamental cradle phone kept on a black three-legged stool. In that era, it was mostly installed at the residence of government employees with the clause of '24 hours' on-call' added to their job description. The telephone lines hanging around a wall bracket on the outside wall of house were a status symbol around the block.

In between his routine of rummaging through the newspaper for job-related advertisements and applying for a score of them, Justin made it a point to routinely peak out of the first-floor window of his house to catch a glimpse of the postman. The postman donning a *khaki* uniform and a Nehru cap would routinely appear on his bicycle to deliver the mail in the neighbourhood. A pile of letters of all sizes would be neatly stacked on the rear carrier of his bicycle, with another bag full of more mail strapped across his shoulder. The postman who always seemed to be in hurry to deliver the mail would—with one swift motion—lean his ride on the wall, pull out the mail from his stack, and drop it in the mailbox. The walls of most houses either had the paint peeled off or had a slight dent made in the place where the postman would lean his bicycle before delivering letters in the mailboxes of different shapes and sizes. Seemingly spotless walls meant the occupants did not get much mail, peeled-off paint showed they received letters every now and then, and a dent in the wall meant that the postman's bicycle frequented that particular house the most.

For the past few days, Justin had been anxiously waiting for a letter from Shelly and at the appointed hour, he would stand at the window though taking care that he may not fall in direct line of the sight of the postman. On a few earlier occasions, while he was waiting at the window, Justin felt very uncomfortable when all of a sudden the postman, while dropping a letter into his mailbox, looked up and met his gaze. Justin felt the man had a meaningful smile on his face, but how would he know that the letter carried love songs from his beloved? Surely, he would not know; it was all in Justin's head, or maybe over the years, the postman was able to discern the contents of the letters, just by gauging the facial expressions of the people awaiting the mail.

That day, as Justin was stealthily peaking from the window, he heard the ring of the bicycle bell of the postman. His heart missed a beat for he knew for sure that there would be a letter for him from Shelly. He rushed down the staircase jumping many steps at a time, unlocked the mailbox and—Yes!—there was a letter for him. He slammed the mailbox shut and ran back up the staircase, again taking many steps in each stride. He took the makeshift letter opener that was his pencil, ripped through the side of the inland letter, closed the door behind him and started reading it. Yes, the light brown mark of Shelly's lipstick making the imprint of her full-blown lips was there! Justin pressed his fingers on the imprint as if touching her lips. After longingly looking at the imprint, he lightly kissed it. He read each word lovingly, sighing and pausing at each endearment and replying to each one of it in his heart. The last part of the letter made his blood rush through his veins, for it said, Shelly was coming to Delhi in the middle of the next week. It was as if his wish had come true.

The four days in between were the longest time Justin had ever waited for anything. He reached the Old Delhi railway station, much earlier than the train was scheduled to steam in. The platform earmarked for the arrival of Jaipur Express was at that point in time occupied by another train, which was preparing to depart.

Now, in those days, the compartments of the trains in India were fitted with cubicle toilets the inside of which had aluminum or sheet paneling. The lower portion of the toilet seat was fitted with an inverted bullhorn pipe to dump the waste on the tracks below. However, the down side was that this inverted drainpipe virtually became a bullhorn, and while the train was moving at full steam, the clanking sound made by the friction between the wheels and the tracks got amplified greatly and could be felt full blast inside the closed cubicle. This reverberating sound at great decibel was not for the meek. A notice was displayed to use the toilet only while the train was in motion and outside the vicinity of a station, in order to keep the platform area free of the offending smell. But many a times, the faint-hearted who could not brave the rumbling sound while the train was moving preferred to use the toilet cubicle while the train was stationary and parked at a platform thus leaving the waste dumped on the tracks open to further petrification and giving rise to 'ghoulish' smell.

The platform was busy, and the peculiar smell, being the 'concoction' of the putrid smell emanating from the tracks and the smell of *puri*[2] and *chole*[3] and *samosa* being deep fried at numerous vending carts hung over the area. Few *coolies* with load

---

2 Fried bread.

3 Chickpeas

of suitcases on their heads and big roll-over sleeping bags, hung over their shoulders, were running the length of the train to lodge their passengers in their respective compartments.

To avoid the chaotic scene, Justin proceeded to the front of the platform where his childhood passion, 'the black steam engine' stood. Majestic in appearance and thoughtfully decorated by the pilot, with brass plates adorning the structure of the boiler and the chimney, the steam engine stood as if waiting impatiently to move forward towards its destination. Hissing and letting off steam, it looked like a big black stallion that was about to gallop on its trail. At the open gate of the cabin, which were fashioned like the arch-gates of some old-fort, stood the pilot of the train. Straining out his neck as far as it would go, to see through a sea of human hands and heads, the 'one hand' of his train conductor, waving a green flag signaling to move the restless black stallion on its onward journey. Getting a synchronised green signal in front and the wave of the green flag by the conductor in the rear, the pilot loosened the reins of the black beast which all of a sudden came to life and started to move forward with lot of hissing and letting off of the steam as if by a dragon. Fascinated even at his age, Justin saw the majestic steam engine move out of the platform with the rest of the train trailing behind.

The track was now clear to receive Shelly's train, the Jaipur Express. Justin did not have to wait too long before he saw the diesel locomotive of Jaipur Express pulling in with its train. The gush of the wind produced by the fast approaching locomotive disturbed the swarm of flies that feasted on and around the tracks. Once again, the platform was filled with the offending concoction. With one hand resting on the side of his head, protecting his hair from being ruffled by the gushing wind that came from the passing train, Justin strained to focus his eyes on the faces that were passing in front of him in quick succession. Loads of people were pressing hard against each other on the now open doors of the train and even more faces pressed harder against the iron grills of the windows, looking out anxiously either for someone who might have come to receive them or trying to signal a porter to carry their luggage.

Spotting someone in a fast moving train is an art. Justin always preferred to stand at a distance to get a wider view, so that he could simultaneously scan many faces that were peering out of the window. However, whatever tactics one employed, there was always a chance that the face one might be looking for would get missed. Keeping his face still, Justin moved his eyes swiftly from side to side, holding in view each compartment that passed by. Suddenly, on catching a glimpse of Shelly's beautiful and equally anxious face, his eyes lit up with joy. He started to run alongside the train holding Shelly's hand and exchanging sweet nothings, which, due to the noise that pervaded the atmosphere, could not be deciphered into intelligent words. The moment the train slowed down a little Justin jumped into the compartment and pushed his way to the cubical where Shelly was standing holding onto her baggage. Justin quickly gave her a light hug and a small peck on the cheek—that is all what the society was prepared to accept in the early seventies. Even that gesture attracted scornful and disapproving looks from the cultured crowd, as if saying not in so many words that such people were the cause of degrading standards of the society. Innocent hugs at such public places could also attract unwanted reaction from the not so cultured and the ruffians that patronised these places, and Justin at 5'7" with 140 lbs. of weight to throw around was not in a mood to encounter any assault from such elements on their turf.

At home, Justin's mother who was otherwise a very humble soul did not feel very comfortable with the idea of an unmarried young girl traveling by herself and coming to stay with them, but she was too gentle and cultured to be vocal about it.

The next two days they visited some common relatives and the third day they kept for themselves. On the third day, once Justin's parents had left for work, Justin and Shelly had the house to themselves. Sitting on the bed holding hands they kept talking and reminiscence about the old days. The long separation was taking its toll, their breathing was heavy and the heat between the two became unbearable. The intimacy that they had missed for a long time was theirs; the pent-up passions became a fury that was promising to consume them completely. It was the first time in three years that the two were in a room with no prying eyes around. The closeness and the privacy they were enjoying slowly led them to an arousal over which they were losing control. Slowly under the sheets, they were devoid of any clothing when Shelly who by then slipped under him spoke something in a muffled voice.

'What, Shelly?' he asked.

'Come', said Shelly with urgency in her voice.

Until now, the two have drawn satisfaction from each other by every other means but had avoided the final act of love-making, which was not only fraught with dangers of unexpected pregnancy but also was something considered proper between husband and wife only. Proper! As if everything going on between them was proper.

Justin was reared in an environment with very clear concept of what was proper and improper, though in that area he could not steadfastly hold onto the 'proper' except for this final act to which Shelly was urging him to initiate and his own flesh also craving hard to attain. Within that split second, while still hanging in the air, Justin made a choice which he could never understand as right or wrong—he did not give in to the urge and denied himself the fulfillment of his own ultimate carnal desire.

That was the last he saw of Shelly. It was as if he lost a part of himself forever.

IVAN

'GOD WRITES YOUR destiny' means one's destiny takes shape according to the laid down principles of the Word of God. That is why even the predestined by God may undergo change of course during their lives based on how they align their actions with reference to the Word. It was predestined for King David of Israel that his kingdom would be an everlasting one. Nevertheless, in conjunction to various actions initiated by him during his life, King David journeyed through the valleys of trial and tribulations before his predestined life could achieve 'the purpose' centuries later, in the coming of the promised 'Messiah' to establish the kingdom.

Psalm 128 speaks about a man who feared God. Sitting quietly in his room, all of a sudden God led Justin to the truth about a man who feared God. His name was Ivan, Justin's father-in-law.

On that fateful day in the early eighties, what intrigued Justin the most was, while undergoing a severe heart attack, Ivan was experiencing more of an emotional trauma rather than the physical pain. Ivan's eyes seemed blank when suddenly Justin caught sight of something in his eyes that spoke volumes. In those moments between life and death, Justin sensed a struggle that this righteous man was undergoing.

Justin experienced a strange phenomenon of life in those

moments, the truth of which he comprehended much later in life, when he himself was in his late fifties.

The Bible says, 'The righteous man walks in his integrity; his children are blessed after him'. (Proverbs 20: 7)

Ivan, Justin's late father-in-law, feared God and the above saying became true in the lives of his sons. His three sons displayed an indifferent attitude towards God but still they started life on a positive note, getting all the worldly blessings for the very reason that their father spent a righteous life.

On the other hand, Justin who by then was in his late fifty's, deduced that in spite of being a minister in the church, he never strictly adhered to God's commandments, for the fear of the Lord is carrying out His commandments with one's might and strength and without reservations. Justin, though convicted at heart on numerous occasions, kept one area of his life closed to any remorse and reproof, and as a result, the principle of the Word of God worked adversely in his life.

Ivan, Justin's late father-in-law, was a frail-bodied man; he had the built of an average Indian male on the outside and a delicate person on the inside. Even though Ivan did not possess eloquent speech and was a man of few words, he was always humble and truthful to the core.

Ivan was dark-complexioned himself but had a very fair and lovely wife named Eugenia, and it could be clearly seen that even after so many years of married life, Ivan was in complete awe of her beauty. Justin noticed that every time Ivan called out his wife by name, his facial expressions and mannerism indicated as though he was enjoying the beauty of a blossoming flower. Eyes gleaming with joy, eyebrows arched up, with mouth slightly open, he would let out a deep 'aah', stretching out the last two syllables of her name to complete his admiration.

Ivan always dressed in white cotton pants and a half-sleeve shirt that was left untucked, the outfit completed by open sandals on his feet. He preferred to walk long stretches rather than take a city bus.

In the evening, one could usually see him standing in his covered balcony on the first floor of his house, overlooking the main road that ran parallel to the colony. This was an exclusive residential area built in the early forties, when people started to move out from the walled city of Delhi, and mostly inhabited by people from Christian faith. The colony had four rows of fifteen houses separated by a service alley. In the evening, the lanes between the rows of houses were full of young children at play. The boys were busy playing cricket or football, while the girls were generally engaged in playing jump rope, hopscotch and so on.

The corner of the colony was landmarked by a church building of red bricks with a steeple that housed the big church bell. No one ever ventured to ring the bell except the sexton, called church *baira* in the local language.

Strangely enough, even though Ivan lived close to that church, he was never its member. He dutifully and without exception attended another Main Line church that was a few miles away from his house in the old city.

Ivan always served as a member of some committee in that church. During the committee meetings, he was not very forceful in expressing himself. His tongue—a bit heavy at the base—did not shape-up like the pointed tip as usually is but was round in the front, which was probably the reason for his sort of gabbled speech. However, his truthful spirit more than compensated the lack of eloquence. He always threw his weight around in favour of the true and the humble. For all of the blessings in his life, he repeatedly said, 'By God's grace'. Every now and then, he repeated this sentence with utmost sincerity and thankfulness to God nodding his head slowly from side to side accompanied by the raising of his hands.

He owned a few shops constructed in the front portion of his house that brought in a steady income as rent. However, he always shied away from going down to collect the rent; so when the shopkeepers approached him instead, to pay the rent, he never failed to express his thankfulness that simply spoke volumes of his humility. His wife, the beautiful Eugenia, was a homemaker and reared his seven children. His was a big family by all standards even in the fifties, four girls and three boys. Ivan and Eugenia named their four daughters after precious stones but such sentiments did not show up while naming the boys. Four out of their seven children took after the mother and were very fair with light hair; the other three took after the father.

That day sitting by himself, Justin remembered his late father-in-law and thought about him in retrospect. It was that fateful evening in the eighties when Ivan was struck by a massive heart attack. In those critical moments, looking deep into the eyes of Ivan, Justin could fathom the emotional trauma and grief that Ivan was undergoing. People in the society valued his word but when it came to dealing with his children, he sounded like a man out of touch with reality. In fact, his older sons were struggling to get a foothold in the world, at the peak of their youth and yet undecided about the vocation to follow. This had created a tense atmosphere in the family, which often proved a recipe for clash of ideas and disagreement. On that fateful day, apparently Ivan could not take it anymore and collapsed. A few days later, he breathed his last in a hospital.

BROTHER ERIC

PORTLY LOOKING AND endowed with spiked hair like a porcupine in its fearful state, 'this man' in his mid-thirties came out of nowhere and started injecting a lot of spirituality into a small group of Christians whom he visited every week. These Christian families were otherwise accustomed to a semblance of a presentation as given by an orchestra conductor of a philharmonic society, which was 'the style' imitated by their Main Line church pastors in conducting the Sunday morning services. The only difference was that in the philharmonic concerts, the symphony or the presentation started in slow, synchronised movements of the players, but by the time the crescendo was reached, the players were immersed in it body, mind and soul, progressing feverishly towards the free expression of emotions through music. Whereas in the church that boasted one of the biggest congregations of the city, the 'players' that were the worshiping congregants remained devoid of any spiritual experience be it the beginning or the end of the service.

In contrast, here was this evangelist called Brother Eric from the state of *Uttar Pradesh*[4] (U.P.) who started conducting Saturday worship services that attracted horde of Christian believers to it. Brother Eric was the man with the complexion of a very well done steak and a resonant voice easily bordering on being

---

4 An Indian State

'hoarse', singing and worshiping as if David himself came down with his harp in the Central Delhi Community Hall.

When Brother Eric was through leading the first half of the Saturday worship service, his face would shine with beads of sweat that got deposited on the contours that textured his face before finally dripping down towards the delta that was his chin. His eyes that were a cross between that of a cat and a fox would gleam in anticipation of an excited response from the worshipers. And what a response he did get! In fact, the worshipers were on a roll-coaster ride of awe and bewilderment before finally landing on the platform of agreement that *this* was the true form of worship. Eric supported his actions and exhortations by quoting verses from his Bible, which was literally in tatters due to overuse. The second half of the worship service, when he brought forth a message from the Bible, was still the more gripping as most of the listeners would be left in a state of amazement. Mouths open and heads nodding in agreement from side to side as they experienced spiritual revelations like never before.

Once the service ended, which was usually short of two hours, someone from the gathering would give Brother Eric a ride on a two-wheeler scooter to the train station to be in his own church in another city the next Sunday morning.

By the end of the fifth week, Justin felt compelled to carry his own Bible to the service; however, the chronological order of the books in the Bible which he had learnt in Sunday school were hard to recall by now. Still Eric, as he was fondly called, would give ample time to the congregants to look up the reference from the index and open their bibles.

JUSTIN & PEARL

JUSTIN, HIS WIFE Pearl, and their son Rahul started attending these worship meetings as conducted by Brother Eric.

After the initial setback to his life by the separation from Shelly, Justin moved on and on a night with near freezing temperatures, when he had joined a Christmas carol singing group, and there he met Pearl. While caroling with the group, he noticed this fair-complexioned girl in her teens singing the soprano part of the carol. Such was her enthusiasm that her cheeks had turned red by the energy she was putting into the singing. Her beauty smote Justin. By now with the history of his past dalliances, Justin had developed his own theory about a relationship that may ultimately culminate into marriage for him. And according to it, he was determined to marry a girl whose beauty would keep him glued to her forever.

He was so sincere about this thought that he approached Pearl, who was virtually unknown to him, and said, 'Will you marry me?' The abrupt straightforwardness of Justin's proposal turned Pearl crimson.

Nervously twisting the scarf around her fingers she said, 'Do I know you?' and quickly mingled with the carolers.

Justin made it a point to get back in her circle during the ensuing Christmas season and after few more encounters, his sincere endeavours were able to break through the damsel's barriers and, thus, started a three-year long period of courtship between the two.

Since meeting Justin, Pearl had successfully dislodged her father Ivan from his favourite place at the first floor balcony of their house. Now every trip of Justin to 'any and everywhere' took a detour onto the road passing in front of her house. Twice a day, he would strap-on his helmet, put on his driving glasses and ride his two-wheeler scooter to go on his pilgrimage—the fair maiden's house. In the beginning, while riding his scooter, Justin would just give a slight nod of his head, and Pearl would acknowledge him with a small wave of her hand. As days passed by, he reciprocated the confident smile on the face of Pearl by intently looking and constantly turning his head in her direction while driving straight ahead, as if presenting a guard of honor to her, army style! The hesitant acknowledgement by the damsel gradually progressed to a more enthusiastic response and Justin felt that, in her own way, she was trying to tell him that she appreciated the attention.

The nod, the hesitant response, the enthusiastic wave all culminated into more close encounters between the two—long before they made life-long commitments to each other. However, history is mute witness to the fact that never have the parents of a fair maiden married off their little princess without spilling bad blood. Justin and Pearl also faced fierce dissidence from her family. Therefore, they got married in a hush-hush way, lest their names were added to the list of immortal lovers such as *Romeo–Juliet*, *Heer–Ranjha*, *Lailla–Majnu*, who were harassed relentlessly by their ancestors until the young lovers gave up their ghost. Nevertheless, those were epic lovers whose saga of love that are staged repeatedly on the Broadway shows still cause people to sigh and cry.

Court marriages in that era were reasons enough to prompt a family-feud that could only be settled on the streets, but Pearl's father Ivan, the man that he was, put a damper on any such ideas that the men-folk of his clan may have entertained.

This is how Justin and Pearl came together to start their family.

SUSHMITA

I T WAS A Saturday and, as it had become customary, Justin, Pearl and their young son had gone to the New Delhi Community Hall where Brother Eric started holding his weekly worship services. Most of the attendees were the erstwhile members from some Main Line church, but all were genuinely interested to give themselves to the new way of worship, as introduced by Brother Eric, and to hear the word from the Bible preached by him in the most exciting and refreshing way. Before Brother Eric preached the Word of God, the worship leader was exhorting the congregation with songs of Praise & Worship, trying to induce some sort of spirituality into the whole atmosphere, or so it seemed. Justin, watching him with amusement, tried to keep his expressions under wraps as he did not want to stand out as an odd man amongst forty and odd congregants.

The worship leader, playing a tambourine, was trying hard to put life and zeal into these people of all ages, invoking their interest in God and His worship. The songs were short choruses with catchy tunes and could make one jump and dance, but no one really moved; the best effort was a forced 'genuine' smile.

For the most, these were new Christian choruses and songs, yet all made an effort to lip sing with the worship leader trying to give an impression that they knew the lyrics. However, efforts to emulate were betrayed by the action of their eyes that were trying to catch the next word of the lyrics on the screen. Though learning this new way of worshipping was quite an effort on the part of everyone present in the meeting, one could see people sincerely trying to get interested in God while singing and trying to move or dance freely in line with the exhortation of the worship leader.

Justin never danced in his life, though the hidden desire was always there to be the best dancer on the floor. His body stiffened while attempting to make any dance moves. It seemed Justin inherited the stiffness from the intense training in his college as an NCC cadet. The cadets marched on the dusty grounds of the college, balancing big rifles with the middle fingers of their left hands. They marched for hours at a stretch, in perfect synchronisation with each other, raising a small cloud of dust each time their heel struck the ground. Trying to sing and move simultaneously during the praise and worship, within the confines of the space in between the seats, Justin found himself vigorously tapping the floor with his heels; only the clouds of dust were missing this time.

Once the worship session was over, all sat down at the behest of the worship leader while he tried explaining a scripture. A few people carried their own Bibles, though no one really knew how and where to open the Bible except for the four gospels found in the New Testament. Justin's wife Pearl was sitting next to him followed by their son Rahul who had still not seen a decade of winters.

The atmosphere was serene and all were listening to the young man with rapt attention when, out of nowhere, a feeble sound of footsteps that constantly grew louder and nearer held Justin's attention. The sound was clearly that of a woman walking with high heel shoes and the pace projected urgency with each step. In the quietness of the hall, the sound of those footsteps grew louder and clearer, until it paused for a split second at the door before entering the hall. As if in synchronisation, many heads turned to look at the person; Justin took care not to literally turn his head but cautiously did throw a glance in the direction of the new entrant. A fair maiden with head held high walked in, dressed in western casuals, with hair cut in layers that were puffed upwards in the front and flowing with each stride. Clutching a small sling-handbag, the damsel sat down next to a middle-aged couple. The congregation that stirred the way a dove puffs up and shakes its feathers for a few seconds before settling down reverted their attention back once again to the young man who was trying to explain eternal life that all need but never really understood.

Brother Eric, who had the Bible on his fingertips, gave the sermon. It touched the hearts of many, out of whom several congregants stood up at the altar call, rededicating their lives to Jesus.

After the service was over, people socialised with each other and met Brother Eric. Justin, along with his wife and son, was moving around trying to meet other members. At the same time, he was discreetly throwing a glance in the direction of the young woman, when all of a sudden, he saw the middle-aged couple with the young woman tagging along, approach Justin and his family. The introduction was appropriate as both families carefully choose the words of salutation to impress each other about the class they belonged. The couple introduced the young woman as Sushmita from the city of Bangalore, and daughter of a distant relative of Mr. Goodwin. She was a software programmer and had come to reside with them as a paying guest. Justin noted the brightness in the eyes of Sushmita; her big brown eyes were expressive and full of excitement. She carried her slender figure gracefully, and punctuated the atmosphere with her laughter every now and then. On the way out, Justin, along with Pearl, joined the elderly couple in the hallway, walking towards the parking lot, while Sushmita took hold of Rahul's hand and walked behind them.

Once in the confines of their cars, Justin and Pearl started discussing the events at the meeting and were happy with the experience, when Justin noted the peculiar fragrance that had permeated the atmosphere inside the car. The perfume was not anything like the one Pearl ever used. Upon scrutiny, it was observed that the source of the fragrance was a bookmark held by their son. Sushmita had given the bookmark dabbed with perfume to their son. The fragrance spoke for itself, it was Chanel.

FAMILY

AFTER THE INITIAL hiccups of the married life, Justin and Pearl were settling down very well, projecting an image of an exemplary couple in their social circle. On social occasions, they generated the vibes of a very happy family, and all admired them for their made-for-each other image.

Justin and Pearl, with their young son in tow, had become regular members of the worship services. The fiery messages sprinkled with some light references always started a murmur in Justin's heart. By nature, and now more so because of being a banker for so many years, Justin responded to many of life's questions with logic and reasoning and, as such, his mind got the better of his heart whenever he felt a tug at it during altar calls.

On many occasions, he invited Brother Eric to his home. There he would have long sessions in the night seeking clarifications and would discuss all those aspects of the Bible, which he blindly believed, because of the childhood teachings of his mother, but could not comprehend for lack of references and a teacher on the subject.

Justin found that this man had detailed, relevant and acceptable explanations to most of his questions, whether they were intelligent, crafty or just plain stupid.

The Main Line Church that Justin used to attend on Sundays had its church building in the old city of Delhi and was a prominent landmark in the area. Its steeple rose majestically high above the surrounding buildings. The structure of the building was taken after the pattern designed for Delhi by Edwin Lutyen, the great British architect known for building a section of the metropolis of Delhi during the *British Raj*.

Inside the main sanctuary, the wall of the altar had a huge stained-glass mosaic pattern depicting resurrected Jesus held in awe by his disciples. The church boasted of one of the finest musical organs in the sanctuary, played by a young organist of great talent and repute. This church where Justin's mother had brought him up and imparted some very important lessons of life was rather dear to him. After attending the Saturday evening worship services, conducted by Brother Eric in the auditorium of the Community Hall, Justin realised that his bond with the Main Line church was more because of the majestic structure of the sanctuary, rather than the spiritual food that he ever received from its pulpit. The serving pastors could never impress Justin beyond their flowing cassocks and pageantry. They lacked the necessary depth when preaching from the Bible, a depth that was evident in messages delivered by Brother Eric.

Each passing day convinced Justin that it was the preaching that made spiritual sense and was instrumental in convicting the spirit. It was after a long time since his teen years that preaching by someone had quickened his heart. However, in spite of this great tug on his heart he held back from responding to any altar call by Brother Eric.

Family Weekends

THE FIRST DAY of the weekend was always a good family day. Justin would take his son Rahul to the nearby playground where they would play badminton or cricket. Meanwhile back at home, Pearl would prepare an elaborate breakfast for the family.

That morning, the dew still lying thick on the grass, the sun glowing like a big red ball, unable to penetrate the mist which hung over the atmosphere, and the birds still hesitant to leave their nests to soar above in the blue sky—Justin had already set up the cricket practice session with Rahul at the play field.

Justin being an over-zealous father wanted his eight-year old son, Rahul, to excel in sports at the school level so he encouraged him to practice with a regular five-and-a-half ounce cricket ball. By now, Rahul had learnt to play some great strokes with straight bat technique. He was learning to attack the ball by quickly stepping out of the crease and at the same time being quick on his back foot to recover his position in the crease. Within an hour of running between the crease and fielding the ball from all over the ground, both Rahul and Justin started sweating when right at that moment, Rahul mistimed a shot and the ball hit his left arm. Doubling up in pain, Rahul threw the bat on the ground while Justin rushed to his side and started rubbing his arm gently. The injury seemed grave and the pain looked excruciating with the skin around the area quickly turning blue. Tears welling up in the eyes of the young boy, they packed up the gear in a huff and rushed towards the house.

The moment they entered the house, Rahul started wailing and the two women in the family, Rahul's mother and grandmother, came running to the child with their motherly instinct writ large on their faces, much to the chagrin of Justin.

Babu, as Rahul was fondly called by everyone at home, did not miss this opportunity to put the blame squarely upon Justin for throwing the ball too fast. Justin with his mouth wide open, due to the sudden accusation by his son in front of his wife and mother, found he was unable to defend himself from the onslaughts of the petite and the fair, who pitched against Justin in favour of Rahul.

Petite in stature was Rahul's grandmother, called *Dadi*, who immediately went running to the kitchen to prepare a homemade remedy called *poultice*[5], made by turmeric paste and few other ingredients spread on a cotton bandage. This she applied on Rahul's arm who was cuddling in the lap of his mother and resisting any advances of reconciliation made by Justin to appease him. The day went by taking care of Rahul, and all the other weekend errands such as laundry, grocery shopping, etc., were put on hold. The afternoon siesta, which was a weekly luxury for Justin, became a taboo that day. By the evening, Justin was in no mood to go and attend the worship meeting and made known his intentions to Pearl of staying home and watching sitcoms.

Pearl, otherwise a mild and non-aggressive person by nature, was always quick to resist any plans to miss the Saturday worship meetings. When Justin tried to be difficult, she announced her intentions of going to the meeting all by herself by hiring a three-wheeler scooter. She played this time-tested trick on Justin for she knew that it was against his nature to let his woman travel alone. There were a few things Justin never felt comfortable for his women folk to do by themselves such as travelling alone, going to a meat shop, taking their son to a barber shop or lifting heavy objects while doing household chores. He was a *ladies first* man and these were not pretensions but were inherent in his nature.

That day, the threat by Pearl to travel by herself had its intended effect. Justin soon got up, and they were on their way to attend the worship meeting. Once at the worship venue, there was no way anyone could sulk or feel withdrawn, as Brother Eric always sprinkled the atmosphere with such genuine happiness and excitement that everyone would become completely involved.

That evening, an elderly man from California, who associated in faith with the Fellowship group, had accompanied Brother Eric. The worship service started and soon built up to a crescendo, which was never a made up thing but something deeper than words could explain.

---

5 Homemade medicinal bandage

In between the worship, the man from California stepped up to Justin laid his hands on him and spoke words of wisdom. In his deep voice he said, 'Thus saith the Lord, you are curious to know me and understand me, and you are trying to do this with your carnal mind; behold, now I do one thing that I open your eyes of understanding and you would know me by faith, and I would use you for my glory'.

Justin felt overwhelmed as well as awkward at the same time—'overwhelmed' because he always felt his body and spirit warring against each other during worship meetings; 'awkward' for he felt many eyes upon him. But that day, the preacher, who did not know him from before, had touched his inner-self.

The sermon that evening was entitled, 'For the Word of God is sharper than any double-edged sword, piercing even to the dividing asunder of soul and spirit'.

Pierced, Justin did get both in soul and in spirit. That evening the trio drove quietly to their home with an occasional interjection of Rahul's childish chatter. That whole week Justin woke up early in the morning to study the Bible in his small makeshift study room. Not knowing as much as where to start reading, he would set the Bible with its spine on the table and randomly read a couple of chapters before getting ready for work. However, he did not seem to comprehend much by reading the Bible in that manner and uneasiness started to build up inside him. By the middle of the week, Justin was not able to take it anymore, so he called Brother Eric and shared his feelings. Brother Eric advised him to start reading the Old Testament and the New Testament of the Bible simultaneously from the beginning. Justin followed the advice and by the time he had finished reading six chapters from the New and the Old Testament of the Bible, Justin felt quickening of his spirit by the word. He kept up his reading for the rest of the week and waited eagerly for the next Saturday meeting.

Justin and his wife were the first to reach the venue and thus helped set up the auditorium of the Community Hall for the worship meeting.

The meeting started with praise and worship songs, and then came the time when Brother Eric invited people for open sharing. At the time when people hesitatingly prepared themselves to come forward and share their testimony, Brother Eric would sing small chorus to fill the void. That day, before Brother Eric could reach the second line of the chorus, Justin felt a strong prompting to go forward with his Bible and share the thoughts he had come to understand during the week.

He stood up and, with a steady stride, reached the podium. Once there, he looked around at the congregation that seemed way different from the participants he had faced many-a-times while attending bank conferences. These were the people not with frowns on their foreheads or raised eyebrows but rather people with expectant and mellow expressions on their faces. They had not come armed with laws and by-laws from the bank's manual, ready to pounce at the slightest opportunity but were people ready to exhort you with Hallelujahs and Amens.

Justin ended his five-minute sharing with a resounding 'Praise the Lord' from everyone. By the time he sat down, he was shaking from head to toe; whether it was apprehension or excitement, he did not know.

Once the meeting was over, Brother Eric excitedly came to Justin and said, 'You brought a very good thought, brother'.

Pearl, who was beaming with joy, suggested that on the way home they should go and eat *kabab* and *roti* at the nearby drive-in, and then they could drop Brother Eric to the train station.

THE GOODWINS

HOSPITALITY WAS THEIR forte and extending it with generosity was their style. They had adopted a culture of pleasing anyone and everyone; sometimes out of pure spirit of friendliness and sometimes, they were making these moves as if on a chessboard.

The man of the house, a burly man in his early fifties with a permanent smirk on his face, had always been a power player in church politics of one of the Main Line churches that they attended until then as a family. Lately, however, he could sense the dwindling court of followers. People were becoming weary of the numerous long-drawn-out court cases that the governing body of the church association had entered into. As a veteran in the game, he knew the thrill from the power game had gone. There were very few players left on the board, and very few occasions came by to put sparkle in his eyes at the 'checkmate' he was so accustomed to calling. Checkmates that were now effectively replaced by the stalemate of inactivity.

In the meantime, the Delhi Christian Fellowship group, the name that Brother Eric had given to the worship services was growing in popularity. This provided the power couple with a new playing field, which did not throw up any active players until then, except for a lone charismatic leader with new insight on the Bible. The exciting worship meetings were in stark contrast to the drab proceedings of committee meetings, which the power-couple were accustomed to attend.

His wife, an executive by occupation, carried herself in a very stately fashion. With a personality that had acquired a few extra pounds over the years, it seemed as if she always walked with each step taken very precisely, firmly gripping the ground to balance her slightly over-rounded frame, which was a few inches shorter from the optimum weight–height ratio for women. Over the years, Mrs. Goodwin was quite fed up with the legal talk that always permeated the atmosphere at her dining table. This was compounded by her dislike for the female participants, without whom the quorum of the meetings could not be met, and one of whom had started private discussions of philosophical nature, unspeakable of in the open, with Mr. Goodwin.

Both, Mr. and Mrs. Goodwin started frequenting the worship meetings regularly. Seated in one of the front rows, Mr. Goodwin would sit in an upright position with the trademark smirk on his face and Mrs. Goodwin sat next to him with a perky countenance that was in total contrast to her matter-of-fact expression, which she carried otherwise. In fact, over the course of time, Justin saw her balancing the two facets, effortlessly.

Very soon, the two became prominent members of the group with the carting, boarding and lodging of Brother Eric, completely taken over by them. This gave Justin a breather and he employed this reprieve to devote more time to pay family visits to the members.

Hospitality

MR. AND MRS. Goodwin were perfect hosts and every Saturday morning, after Brother Eric's arrival from the train station, they would lay a kingly breakfast. At the breakfast table, Brother Eric with his eloquent speech in chaste Urdu language with fair sprinkle of 'migratory' Persian words and a topping of English spoken with an Australian accent would leave everyone around struck with amazement and amusement.

The light-hearted moments at the breakfast table were followed by visits to a few important people that Brother Eric was trying to draw into the group. Visiting the other lesser mortals was the responsibility of Justin.

For the purpose of visitation, Brother Eric preferred being driven in the car by Mrs. Goodwin, as she scored higher on safe driving compared to her husband, whose driving style gave the impression as if he was dodging a guided missile following his car close behind. Every time Mr. Goodwin got behind the wheels of his car, he would grin ear to ear. His eyes would have a gleam of expectancy to hear thankful praises from whoever was travelling with him in the car, for his 'James Bond' style driving created a scenario as if the occupants had just escaped certain destruction at the hands of some sneaky invisible missile that followed the car. The lack of appreciation for his skills was not treated kindly, and the accompanying passenger, who undoubtedly would be completely shaken up by the ride, risked being off-loaded midway with an excuse of some very urgent business that seemed to come up all of a sudden. Still, he was the best person around, and whenever there arose an occasion where something needed to be done at the shortest notice, Mr. Goodwin was the obvious choice. No one could beat him at that, and he took pride in it and rightly so.

Their individual talents, unflinching loyalty and unquestioned availability at all times were a great asset for the church work. However, at the same time, their slightly uncompromising approach and less-than-accommodating attitude for others in general were an impediment to the freedom of spirit in the Lord's work. Brother Eric, however, ignored the negatives and instead harnessed the potential of the abilities of this husband and wife duo towards furtherance of the church work.

THE CALL

THE CHURCH WORK started to grow in number and commitment by the people, and there were talks of starting a Sunday morning church service. Justin, who earlier did not favour this idea, now was the main proponent of starting the Sunday morning church services by the group. This was because after the Saturday night spiritual feast, attending the Sunday service in a Main Line church became less fruitful, and Justin started feeling that it was not benefiting him or his family in any way. Many others, who started attending these worship services regularly, were still not prepared to leave their age-old association with the Main Line church; however, for of most them, the Sunday service in their respective churches was becoming more of an increasingly hollow experience, especially after the vibrating spirit-filled services of the Delhi Christian Fellowship group. For this reason, slowly, many members were getting around the idea of starting the Sunday morning church services.

Justin was continuously growing in the understanding of the Word. At his work place in the bank, he always kept his Bible open in the upper right drawer of his desk, enabling him to make a quick reference to it whenever a particular thought enlightened him.

In the evening, he would ride his motorcycle and visit a few fellowship members, praying and fellowshipping with them.

Many-a-times, Pearl would accompany him on such visits. With each passing day, more and more people requested him to come and visit them during the week. During such visits, the whole family would gather round him and lend their ears to whatever he shared with them from the Bible, giving Justin the feeling of an extended family.

Justin's involvement in church activity was increasing on a daily basis, to the extent that he exhausted all his leave at the bank while attending the church work and at other times, just staying back at home to dwell on the Word. He started to get many opportunities to preach the Word in the worship meetings and it always proved to be a very exciting experience. The Bible started opening up to him in a very new way; practically every other verse he read caught his attention, and these were no imaginations but revelations that he started feeling in his spirit.

Soon it became apparent that Justin was not able to do justice to his work at the bank and the church simultaneously. He had never been casual with any of his responsibilities. As a result, a time had come when he needed to decide to engage himself fully with one task and quit the other. He and Pearl got down on their knees to pray for guidance on the subject and after much prayer, they arrived at the conclusion that Justin needed to quit the bank job and get into full-time ministry with the church. The conviction was complete and total and as such, there were no second thoughts or hesitation of any kind.

They shared their thoughts with Brother Eric, who strengthened their resolve with his support. Slowly, they started spreading the word amongst friends and relatives. Most of them, however, disapproved of leaving such a nice job and moving into full-time ministry.

'What will happen of your children?'

'You both are young and have got a long way to go'.

'How would you meet the expenses? The church will not be able to substitute the salary and all other perks that the bank provides'—these were just a few among the many thoughts shared by his friends and relatives.

His colleagues from the bank, most of whom were from different faith could never comprehend his decision.

Justin's resolve and Pearl's support did not waiver with all this discouraging talk. Rather, with resolute firmness, they started their journey of faith; and finally Justin resigned from the bank.

The people in the church circles, though still trying to comprehend the move, were nevertheless awe struck by the boldness of it all.

Brother Eric was not only a very close observer of all spiritual moves that were happening within his group, but was also a very good planner to handle and prepare in advance for such matters. Justin was leaving his job to be in full-time ministry and the church members were excited and ready to be a part of it all.

Brother Eric encouraged all for the establishment of a church base in Delhi. Contributions were raised to rent and equip a place as an assembly hall on the ground floor, along with an office and a small room on the first floor to facilitate short stays by visiting ministers. The rented premises underwent renovation, and soon, the Delhi Christian Fellowship group had an assembly hall with all the furniture and equipment that goes into the making of a serene worship place.

Justin and Pearl were excited by the prospects of their group having a designated place of their own for worship services. God was rewarding their walk of Faith.

TODDAR MALL

AFTER WORKING FOR more than a decade and half, Justin left his bank job. Before finally vacating the bank apartment, he started making rounds of property brokers to look for a rental house. When in the bank, Justin found these property brokers to be very friendly and overtly eager to assist in locating a suitable property for rent. For the purpose, while negotiating with the property owner, they would go out of their way to vouch for Justin, though they hardly knew him personally. It always amused him to see these people talking with extra politeness that certainly betrayed their otherwise boisterous mannerisms.

Justin entered the office of one of the property brokers in the neighbourhood to probe the prospects of finding some property for rental stay. Seated behind a large burgundy-coloured executive table was this hefty man wearing an equally, and appropriately, thick gold chain around his neck. Another gold chain, of the same size, dangled loosely from his wrist, the fingers of which had more stone-studded rings than the count of them. Occasionally, he would tap the table with the ring of his thumb to the tune of some song from a Bollywood movie. An underage boy, illegally employed by the property dealer to carry out odd jobs, was seated on the stool near the entrance, always alert and ready to jump to the commands of his master. Two huge, garland-laden photo frames with photographs of some gurus hung from the wall behind the desk. The heavy smell of rose and cinnamon filled the room from the burning of the *agarbatti* (incense sticks) that were stuck in the two lower corners of the frames.

On seeing Justin standing at the door, the tapping fingers stopped in mid-track and a smile spread corner-to-corner on the face of Toddar Mall. He could not ignore the very noticeable gleam in Toddar Mall's eyes that sent a clear signal to Justin as if he were a sheep standing in front of his shearer. Very enthusiastically, he welcomed Justin and sent the little boy scurrying around to fetch two cups of tea.

After the exchange of pleasantries, Justin stated the purpose of his visit that was received well by Toddar Mall who said, '*Saheb*[6], how many years lease your bank would like to sign?'

'Toddar Mall *ji*[7], I am working no more for the bank. I have resigned from there and now I am a Pastor'.

'You have resigned from the bank!' was the cry in disbelief. 'So what are you now, you said … err?' he continued with confusion writ large on his face.

Justin forced a smile and clarified again that now he was a Pastor, which means he was a minister in a church.

'Minister!' jettisoned Toddar Mall, 'Oh, when did you become a minister?'

Shifting uncomfortably in his chair, with a smirk on his face and at his wit's end, Justin found himself at loss of words to explain his present vocation to this thick-skinned blockhead.

At the very moment, as if to give Justin some reprieve, Toddar Mall himself interjected one more time, 'You mean, Father *ji*?'

'Yessss!' Justin gave out a sigh of relief and slumped back in his chair. It took a few moments for the air of confusion to clear.

---

6 Form of addressing a man respectfully

7 Showing respect while calling someone by name

'I do not deal in renting of apartments anymore', replied Toddar Mall; this time Justin nearly fell off the chair.

Justin took some time to change his jaw-dropping expression into a more acceptable one and said, 'But just now you were asking me about the period for house lease!'

'I did say, but the property owners do not prefer to enter in lease except with banks or companies, sorry, *muaf-karna*[8] *ji.*' Toddar Mall shouted to the little boy '*Oye chotu*[9]*!* Can you clear the table?' Justin quickly realised the 'discussion over' signal and took his leave.

Boy! He was glad to come out of Toddar's office! 'Err...' does not have any meaning in the Hindi language, but addressing Justin with a heavy emphasis on the last syllable of the word 'Pastor' was like making an 'error' out of him. Justin was furious and wanted to beat the crap out of him, but hey! he stopped himself from entertaining any further insults for this man. Being a pastor now, he should not even entertain such thoughts or play with such expressions in his mind. On top of it, he was no Hercules; he would not even attempt to manhandle that hefty Toddar Mall.

He remembered this old incidence that happened in his early years. Justin had never entered physical street bout with anyone except that one time while he was studying in grade three when a fat bully challenged him to fight for whatever reason. He accepted the challenge in the most macho way of an eight-year old. Justin with his challenger walked to the school playing field followed by a group of cheerleaders from both camps.

The fight started amidst loud cheering from the two sides and both the warriors lunged at each other. Even the supporters from each camp started a virtual fight of their own. Flailing their hands in the air, and literally pushing and hitting the opponent

---

8 An expression used for 'Sorry'

9 A general expression for a young male servant

in their fast-paced wild actions, the chaotic groups surrounded the two gladiators. Then, all of a sudden, Justin tumbled and fell with the fatso falling over him. That was it! You see, there are advantages of being fat too. Justin tried pushing away that dead weight from top of him, but to no avail. Pinned under his weight, Justin threatened the fatso with dire consequences, and at each such threat, the fatso chose to jump upon him. Luckily, for Justin, the school bell rang signalling the end of the lunch recess. Immediately, supporters from both the camps vanished as if in thin air, leaving the two warring opponents walking side-by-side to their classes. From that day, Justin developed a phobia of fatsos, and certainly not today, he wasn't prepared to err and get into a brawl with this ... well!!

Walking back home, one fact dawned upon Justin that owners of apartments would not be too keen to enter into a lease with him—now *that* was troublesome.

Pearl, without any apprehension, was waiting to hear some positive news when Justin dampened her spirit by explaining the scenario. They decided that it would be best to tell the one who is going to employ Justin. Therefore, they both got down on their knees and prayed to God about their predicament. It was not like that immediately there was a knock on the door with a property dealer standing and offering them a house on lease, but they surely got encouraged once again.

Time was flying by at super speed and the day to vacate the bank apartment was drawing close. Sometimes things do not dawn upon someone until they face a real life situation. Justin just realised that, except for their personal belongings, all other things in the house—from curtains to carpet, sofa-sets to dining-tables, refrigerators to air-coolers—were provided by the bank and once they vacate the house, they would not be left with any furniture and other necessities. They now needed to buy all these things by themselves and once they do that, Justin's retirement funds would deplete to an unsafe level.

Eventually, they found a nice, reasonably priced house on lease, and God arranged for the lease papers so miraculously, that Pearl's company, which never entered into house-lease on behalf of employees, started with her as the first case. Both saw the hand of God in it and were greatly encouraged.

The bank gave a warm send off to Justin in appreciation of his services that spanned over sixteen years working at different branches, all the while rising in cadre and holding important portfolios.

WALK OF FAITH

J USTIN NEEDED TO furnish the house from scratch and he had to dip heavily in the retirement funds that he got from the bank. To balance the investment, Justin bought a three-piece sofa set from a used furniture store, which was summarily rejected by Pearl. Justin scurried back to the store to return it and incurred a loss. With great reluctance, Pearl hung the cheap quality curtains that Justin had bought.

Scaling down one's standard of living is not easy, even though it was only in the nature of a slightly more compact house with fewer amenities. Nevertheless, after the initial teething problems, they started to learn to adjust in their new situation. It was faith ministry after all, which meant there was no definite income pattern or a fixed salary from the newly formed church. As per Justin's calculation, the retirement funds would have seen him through to the next coming year. However, to keep up with the need to visit the church families on a regular basis, he had to dig deeper in his pocket to finance his travel and very soon, this made the funds deplete faster than expected. Still Justin never scaled down his visitation. He knew for sure that God had called him for His ministry, and as such, He would make a way for him.

The revelations that he constantly got from reading the Bible made his life very exciting, and by now, he got more opportunities to share in the church services on a regular basis. Brother Eric started concentrating on other centers and reduced his visit to Delhi to twice a month. This gave Justin great exposure with the congregation and the members started relating more with him. The congregants would treat him as a family member whenever he visited them and would share all their family matters without any inhibitions. He felt as if now he had a big extended family that demanded his attention the same way his own family did. People started looking forward to his visits and many would not make decisions concerning their family matters without consulting him.

Justin used to start his day very early in the morning; he would take a cup of tea and with his bible would go into a small five-by-six foot room that served as a study room. By seven, Rahul, his elder son, would catch his school bus and by eight, Pearl would leave for her job with a multinational company. Justin would then spend some time with his younger son, Armaan, who was two years old by then.

SUNITA CHANDRA

WITHIN A COUPLE of years, when both the boys started to go to school, Justin started to have ample time to himself before the evening set in. Giving much time to read the Bible and spend time in prayer was now his prime interest. He would sit down with his Bible and make notes on all the thoughts that kept enlightening him from time to time. This was a new experience and each new revelation from the Bible would enthrall him. Every day, he eagerly waited for such afternoons until it was time for him to pick up his sons from the school bus stop.

At the bus stop, Rahul would alight first, followed by a beaming, five-year old Armaan, who would take small-but-quick steps to run into Justin's arms. Immediately thereafter, Armaan would start his story session, rounding up all the happenings in the school that would continue non-stop until they reached home, which was a mere five-minute walk from the bus stop. The trio, along with Justin's mother, would then sit down for evening snacks and fruits, followed by some games and then study-time for the boys. By evening, Pearl would also join everyone in the family activities and by dusk, Justin would go out to make pastoral visits to some of the church families.

That evening, Justin crisscrossed the city of Delhi, visiting some families living on the other end and returned rather late in the night.

In the third watch of the night, when people drift into a deep slumber or are enjoying a pleasant dream, Justin's phone broke the silence of the night with its shrill ring. He jumped out of the bed with a start and reached quickly for the phone to ensure that the ring did not disturb others in the house.

'Hello', he said in a hushed voice, covering the mouthpiece with the curvature of his palm to minimise the sound.

'Hello, brother', was a feeble response of a woman on the other side.

Justin looked at the wall clock; its iridium hands showed that the time was 2 am.

'Who is it?' narrowing his eyebrows, he asked again.

'Brother, this is Sunita Chandra', was the response. 'I am very disturbed and cannot sleep, could you please come and pray for me'.

After thinking through it in his mind, Justin said, 'Okay, I will come, give me some time'.

Pearl, who was a light sleeper, had woken up by then and asked, 'What happened?'

Justin was always a man of few words except when he was preaching or discussing the Bible with someone, so his explanation was short and to the point, conveying at the same time that he would have to go to Mrs. Sunita Chandra's house and that she should go back to sleep.

It took him slightly more than a quarter of an hour to reach the DDA colony where Sunita Chandra lived. Night travel at such an hour was fraught with many dangers, one of which was to avoid the self-appointed guardians of the colony—the stray dogs. These custodians would embark to patrol their territories in the night and furiously follow any intruder who dared to venture there. Travel on a motorcycle was even riskier because the noise that the two-stroke engine made would immediately catch the attention of such guardian dogs who, on seeing the rider, would run alongside the two-wheeler barking and baring their fangs. Justin was praying to avoid any such encounter. He reached the colony that had many blocks of four-story buildings made up of one-bedroom apartments. Originally built by the Delhi Development Authority, all apartments were of the same design from the outside, generally painted with grey colour. However, the colony that was now more than two decades old had undergone a complete transformation undertaken haphazardly by the occupants of various apartments. Most of the occupants had extended their balconies beyond the authorised plan, thus converting the one-bedroom into three or even four-bedroom apartments, and in the process compromising the structural safety of the whole block.

Justin started looking for a place to squeeze-in his motorcycle and park it in between a fleet of scooters, motorcycles and bicycles which were parked any and everywhere. People had a tendency to park their vehicle closest to the staircase and many-a-times, one had to jump over the front wheel of such two-wheelers to get to the first step of the stairwell. Incidentally, and to Justin's surprise, the stairwell in this block was nicely lit but the excessively depilated steps and the peeling paint on the walls stood a mute witness to the absent upkeep of any kind.

On reaching the apartment of Sunita Chandra, Justin paused for a few minutes to comb his hair and clean his face, which would have caught the soot that hung around this industrial area, and then pressed the doorbell.

Sunita Chandra, a woman in her mid-forties with a physique that trumpeted her enmity with any regimen of physical exercise except that of climbing the flight of steps to her third floor apartment, opened the door. After the pleasantries, that were too much to ask for at that hour of the night, Justin settled down in the sofa-chair in this otherwise nicely kept apartment.

'So, Sunita *ji*, what happened?' Justin asked with concern in his voice. 'Is everything fine with you?'

These few words of sympathy by Justin were enough to break loose the dam of sorrow that had lately engulfed her life. Sunita Chandra had been leading a rather hard life, with not much emotional support from anyone. After the death of her husband, she was now living with her only son on whom she was pinning all the hopes of her life. However, the relations between the mother and the son, who was in his twenties, had strained because of their daily clashes on trivial matters. The disagreement reached such proportions that her son decided to walk out on her. Justin was aware of the situation and was already in contact with the son, who with some prayer and persuasion had agreed to move back with his mother.

By then, Justin had understood that Sunita Chandra did not face any new situation of great concern, and it was because of her depressed feelings that prompted her to call Justin at this unearthly hour of the night. However, at that time, just listening to her woes would help her regain her composure. That is exactly what Justin did.

While on his way back, he thought in retrospect that this all makes a part of his Pastoral ministry. People would wake you up, for they themselves cannot sleep.

RAGHUNATH MASSEY

DELHI, THE BIG metropolitan city and the capital of India, had an ever-increasing population that attracted migratory populace both from far and near.

On the Southeastern border of the city runs the famous *Yamuna* river that has on its banks, the famous *Lal Qila*[10] built in 17th century by the Mughal Emperor Shah Jahan. This was the last bastion of the Mughal Empire against the ever-expanding *British Raj* that started to spread its tentacles after the battle of Plassey in Bengal, defeating the *Nawab*[11], *Siraj ud-Daulah*.

A majestic and by now a century-old bridge called the *Yamuna* Bridge, built by the Britishers, connected Delhi to the state of *Uttar Pradesh*. Until the early sixties, *Yamuna* river was considered sort of an outer limit for the city of Delhi. Many-a-times, while visiting and standing on the ramparts of *Lal Qila*, Justin had seen this bridge. Its huge structure, which spreads across the width of the *Yamuna* river, always fascinated Justin's imagination as a young boy.

It was out-of-bounds for Justin to traverse this bridge; however, once Justin's curiosity got the better of him and without telling anyone, he decided to venture across it on his bicycle. Even in the sixties, the bridge attracted heavy traffic—its lower span used

10 Famous Red Fort in Delhi, India

11 Title for a ruler of princely states in India before independence

by cars, interstate buses, trucks and bicycles, all running neck and neck with each other. The bicycle riders were either the people commuting to work to industries and other establishments on both sides of the bridge, or they were milk vendors carrying milk in heavy aluminum containers hanging by the hooks attached on either sides to the rear carrier of their vehicle. Justin's venture on the bridge travelling out of the city was adventurous and incident-free. He enjoyed the thrill a teenager gets when on such forays without the knowledge of his elders, however risky it may prove to be. Young people get a sense of accomplishment and feel feathers added to their name when undertaking such feats. While making the return trip on the bridge, Justin, beaming with excitement and basking in his own glory, was riding his bicycle with many milk vendors riding in front and behind him as well. As luck would have it, Justin's sparkling eyes suddenly caught the sight of his father traveling in a company car just ahead of him. Justin's brain froze and his natural reflexes made him instantaneously jam the brakes of his bicycle. The traffic in front just kept going but all hell broke loose behind him...

The cyclists, most of whom were milk vendors carrying big containers filled with gallons of milk, hit Justin's cycle and one after another, a row of bicycles fell on the road. In the process, their milk containers hit the road and with the lids flying loose, gallons and gallons of milk spilled on the roadside. There was a big commotion and a lot of confusion, for a few seconds; no one understood how and why everything happened. However, once the initial shock was over, the big burly villagers riding those bicycles were all over Justin screaming '*Oye*! *Cycle kyun roki?*' ('Why did you stop the bicycle?'). It was only his young age, which saved him from being thrashed that day.

The Dumping Ground

THE STRETCH OF land on the other side of the bridge towards the borders of U.P. extended another fifteen miles and was sparsely populated. Even in the early sixties, Delhi, which was densely populated, always faced a massive problem of disposing off the daily refuse. Therefore, the government of the Union Territory of Delhi decided to use the low-lying areas around the *Yamuna* river and this fifteen-mile stretch along the G.T. Karnal Road as a dumping ground. As a result, a strong stench along the G.T. Road hung permanently.

After graduating from school and a few years from the initial debacle of his adventurous journey on the *Yamuna* Bridge, Justin got to ride these roads on a regular basis. On completion of high school, Justin got a summer job with *Rajpal and Sons*, a paperback publisher situated on G.T. Karnal Road. He now rode his bicycle every day to his work place. While coming back in the evening, he had to travel on the side of the road where the city dumped its pilling refuse. The nearly three-mile journey on that road used to be a voyage through hell. Because of the putrefying garbage, the area was a breeding ground for flies, insects, bugs and more bugs. Every cyclist riding through that area needed to cover his or her face with a handkerchief or piece of cloth. It was also essential that one's shirt be completely buttoned-up and sleeves needed to be rolled down. Wearing elastic bands around the cuffs of trousers too was a lifesaver from the onslaught of the army of insects that swarmed the whole area. All these precautions were essential to save cyclists from the bugs that would otherwise creep inside their clothes. However, the riders would still get completely invaded by them on the outer surface of their clothing.

Another scenario, which horrified cyclists on this track, was when a garbage tractor-trailer drove in front of them. With the filth loosely covered by a trampoline and its free end (there was never a tractor-trailer with all four ends tied properly) wildly flapping in the air, the garbage carried by the vehicle used to—literally—fly in the face of the cyclist that followed behind.

The Bible says that in hell, there would be crying and gnashing of teeth, but here on this side of G.T. Karnal Road, one dare not open the mouth to cry or gnash his teeth lest it be filled with bugs and flying garbage. Disgusting ... every evening the bicycle ride used to be nauseating and stomach-turning.

By the time the eighties rolled in, the situation had completely changed. There now stood rows of newly constructed buildings on that stretch of the dumping grounds.

The cycle riders of the seventies had almost become extinct, with their place effectively taken over by the fast-moving and zigzagging two-wheeler scooter, and the typical *phat-phatias*, the smoke-spewing monsters of the eighties. Vehicular smoke, which eternally hung in the area, had effectively replaced the earlier stench of the bygone era.

Pastor Raghunath Massey

ON THIS SIDE of *Yamuna* lived Raghunath Massey who was the newest addition to the Delhi Christian Fellowship group that by now had established its presence in the city for nearly five years.

Pastor Massey was an urbanite with a rustic look. Working in the city corporation office, he had a permanent greasy look on his forehead. His lisp, when pronouncing the letter 'h', gave rise to many stand-up comedians in the church, who took pleasure in mimicking this Pastor behind his back.

Outwardly, the senior circle of pastors and ministers that included Brother Eric, Pastor Bose, the Goodwins and Justin himself, discouraged these jokesters but when left to themselves, they could not resist the temptation of having some hearty laughs.

Raghunath Massey treated the seniors with a smile while his juniors always had to be content with his serious side. He would be most attentive to the suggestions and opinions of his seniors and would easily resolve to agree with the consensus; however, by the time such decisions needed implementation, his earlier resolve would shift altogether in a different direction floating towards his own ideas, overriding the earlier show of unanimity.

The congregation in his church liked Justin very much as a speaker, and as such, on many occasions, he went there to preach. On that particular Sunday also, Justin was well received by the congregation. After the service was over and people had dispersed, Raghunath Massey took Justin and Pearl to a member of the church who was still waiting for them.

The woman member was suffering with severe spondylitis of the neck. The problem was so severe that she was unable to move her neck without experiencing excruciating pain. Justin and Pearl, along with Pastor Massey, laid their hands on the woman. Justin prayed in the name of Jesus, rebuking the pain to leave the woman to which all responded with an affirmative 'Amen'. They had prayed with great faith but Justin could not gather the courage to ask the woman as to how she felt; and no one broached upon the subject directly. After some time, Justin and Pearl left Raghunath Massey's place and drove to their home.

On reaching their house, Justin's mother told him that Pastor Massey had called a few times and had requested them to call back, as soon as possible.

'Brother, Praise the Lord', was the first sentence that Raghunath Massey said excitedly on receiving the returned call from Justin.

'Brother, the woman you had prayed for is healed. After you two had left, the woman had some fellowship with my wife and while she was talking, she felt that she was able to move her neck freely and the excruciating pain was gone'.

Justin and Pearl immediately went down on their knees and thanked God for His hand of mercy.

God was stretching forth His hand to give them an increase in their Church ministry.

ASSEMBLY HALL

THE SUMMERS IN Delhi can be very punishing at times, with temperatures during the season generally soaring as high as 45°C. The two-floor building where the Assembly hall for the church services of Delhi Fellowship Group was taken used to become extremely hot by virtue of getting direct sunlight on its rooftop. Air conditioners were a luxury; however, the office room attached to the Assembly hall was fitted with an air-cooler. Justin enjoyed the solitude the place offered for his Bible studies, along with a good work environment.

The church office was close to the house where Sushmita was staying as a paying guest with the Goodwins. A native of the city of Bangalore, she had come down to Delhi to join a software firm as a junior programmer. She had odd working hours, from 3 pm to 11 pm, and as such had plenty of time on her hands during the day. On one such day, she came to the church office while Justin was setting up the new computer system. She, being in software programming, proved to be of much help in setting up the system.

The church had completed five years in the city, and now Justin was leading it as a full-time pastor. To commemorate the completion of five years, it was decided that a church brochure be published. Sushmita, though a new member of the church, got involved in the project in a big way as she had earlier experience of attending such jobs at her previous work place in Bangalore. She was also in a position to daily spare her time until the afternoons, and this extra help was more-than-welcome by Justin. Each day, Sushmita and Justin would huddle together for hours discussing threadbare every aspect of the brochure.

Justin found Sushmita to be very well informed and bright, and her creativity was giving the brochure a very exciting look. Slowly, Justin started enjoying Sushmita's presence, which was like a whiff of fresh air punctuated with tons of laughter and many lighter moments. Justin found her company to be very invigorating and on many occasions, they would drift from the subject of the brochure and talk on unrelated subjects for hours together.

That day, the intense heat at that early hour gave the feeling as if the sun was rising with a vengeance, moving across the sky with a purpose to scorch the helpless inhabitants of the city. Hot winds were blowing and on the block of the DDA flats where Justin lived, every blast of the wind caused small whirlwinds to rise up, in a conical shape, from the ground to the top of the five-storied buildings, carrying with it dust and any small litter that was around.

Justin was keen to go to the church office, as a lot remained to be done for the publication of the brochure. Once on the road and riding on his motorcycle, he felt the full blast of the hot air that was blowing around. The dust picked up by the wind would hit him on the face like tiny specks of molten lava. It was a torturous task even the more, to ride next to a passing city bus or truck, as the exhaust would make one feel as if passing through a furnace. The tar on the roads had melted in many places and had gathered in layers near the stoplights where the heavy vehicles applied their brakes to come to a stop. The uneven surface of the road at such intersections made the ride bumpy and braking more difficult. Braving all this, Justin rode his motorcycle the few kilometers that was between his house and the church office.

Once there, he took no time to park his motorcycle on the side road and hastened to unlock the main gate. To his surprise, the main gate was already unlocked. Justin also noticed that the lights in the church office at the first floor were on and the big air-cooler was running making the room temperature several degrees lower than the outside temperature.

Baffled and hesitant, Justin stepped into the office room and called out, 'Hello?'

'Hello', came the reply in the same tone followed by the emergence of Sushmita from the kitchen with her long hair gathered up carelessly in a bun.

'Hey, how come you are so early today?' asked Justin, suppressing his amused expression with a smile.

'Just like that', was Sushmita's reply. 'It was so hot so I thought how about making the work place cool by running the air-cooler before we settle down for work?'

Justin also noted the aroma of omelets coming from the small kitchen that had not been put to any use until now. With a smile and question on his face, Justin looked inquiringly towards Sushmita.

'That is a surprise for you, how about you freshen up first?'

Today was an exceptionally hot and dusty day and Justin felt as if each pore of his face was covered with grit, so he quickly proceeded to the bathroom to freshen up. Within minutes, he was out, all fresh and bright. By then, Sushmita had laid the breakfast table and was standing there with a wide smile upon her face. Oh! This was the surprise. Well, some light snacks before the start of the work was not a bad idea.

For a brief moment, Justin's eyes noticed the beauty of this young maiden, something which he had not taken note of before; however, with same abruptness, he took his mind off from any such thoughts. He sat down at the breakfast table that she had laid and started discussing the progress of the brochure. Trying hard to concentrate on the work and not let his mind wander, he was not beside himself that day. They ended the work much earlier than usual. Sushmita left with a confused expression not understanding the sudden change in Justin's countenance.

DEEPAK RASTOGI

HIGHLY EDUCATED AND very well placed in his career, Deepak Rastogi had a physique, which was perfectly described by Ernest Hemingway in his novel, *The Old Man and The Sea*, as a man who was 'thin and gaunt with deep wrinkles'. The Indian version of the character, Deepak, endowed with all the above, had bespectacled sunken eyes and sported a beard like that of a 'billy goat'. His bodily presence was weak but his speech was weighty and powerful. By nature, he would go to the extent of expressing his happiness with small chuckles and always stop short of a hearty laughter. During discussions, one would find him intently staring into empty space, which, in turn, would lead him to a philosophical explanation of the matter. Deepak was a friend, guide and philosopher to all his simple hearted congregants, who strived hard to follow the lead of the spirit. He in turn afforded them the protection like that of a firewall from carnal-minded outside forces. He was a small man with big dreams. His associates would flock around him as if around a *Guru*, and his adversaries would keep themselves at arm's length for fear of consenting with him per force of his spiritual explanations, put up in a very literary way and, at times, beyond their comprehension. Fondly known as 'Brother Deepak', in his church circle, he spoke chaste Hindi in a Shakespearean way and conversed in Queens English with an Indian accent.

Deepak was a very good musician with mastery in playing a number of instruments and a voice that somehow seemed to echo from the space above and travel back to the listener, penetrating the very dividing line of soul and spirit. Justin's association with him had stood the test of a few summers. That evening, Justin, with his wife and two sons, was driving down to preach in Deepak's Fellowship meeting, held every Sunday evening on the open terrace of his house. The evening sky on that Sunday in July was heavy with dark clouds and lightening striking at regular intervals. On the road, every clap of thunder would force people to stare at the threatening clouds above and quicken the scramble to reach their abode. The sky witnessed stray crows, which were late in flight to roost in the tree of their choice, now shooting down with urgency from one tree to another, so as not to be caught in the imminent downpour.

Once at Brother Deepak's place, Justin found most of the active members in a frenzy preparing to face the inevitable heavy downpour. Pearl looked at Justin to assess his reaction but seeing his composed exterior, she drew confidence to herself and without a word exchanged, she knew the storm would pass and they would experience God's goodness that evening.

During the meeting, at each rumble and grumble of the clouds accompanied by the howling easterly wind, the congregants that assembled on the open terrace would flinch and steal a quick look at the clouds above. However, the unwavering confidence, displayed by Deepak and Justin, who were leading the prayer meeting, raised the bar for others also and soon enough they all started feeling comfortable in the face of the continued inclement weather. Braving the weather defiantly, the meeting ended with prayers offered for various needs.

Before departing, Justin inquired about the wellbeing of Deepak's mother and was told that she was sick and was in a room downstairs. They went down to meet and pray for her. At the very first sight of her, Justin recoiled within himself but quickly steadied his steps. The appearance of the skin on her forearm was like that of the bark of a tree and Justin came to understand that it was due to an advanced stage of eczema that she had. Such things always repulsed Justin, as by nature, he could not behold such a sight. However, at that time, Justin overcame his initial shock and stepped forward to pray by laying his hands on Deepak's mother. The group prayed fervently to God to stretch forth His hand and heal the sick of such a formidable looking disease.

HEALED

GOD WAS BLESSING Justin with mighty words and the congregation was benefiting by it in their daily life. People were growing in spiritual understanding; the name of their church had become well known in the Christian circle of the city of Delhi.

It was more than three weeks when he had gone to preach in Deepak's church when he received a call from him.

'Brother Justin', said Deepak from the other side.

'Yes', he said, answering Deepak's call.

'Brother, there is some good news. My mother has healed completely. The scales on her arm are falling off and new skin is appearing in its place'.

'Praise the Lord, brother! God is honoring you as a minister of His word by taking away the sickness of your mother'.

Believers in the sister churches joyfully received the news, for Deepak was a well-known minister.

Such incidents were on the rise and as a result, many new members were coming to the fold of Delhi Christian Fellowship group that had grown to six branches in the city of Delhi.

Learning God's will

THERE WAS A woman, a very devout believer who was also a committed member of Justin's church and was sick for some time. After detailed medical diagnosis, news came that she had breast cancer. Justin, with the church prayer group, prayed for her continuously. However, due to her deteriorating medical condition, the doctor advised for immediate surgery followed by a long spell of chemotherapy. In the long run of his ministry, this incidence made Justin accept the will of the Lord, making him more humble. He learnt many phases of God's mercy that manifested in various forms, which were healing as answer to prayers, miraculous healing, gift of wellbeing, provisions and sometimes even the absence of an answer to the prayers. Justin was learning that God was sovereign and has a plan and purpose for every life that many a times is beyond the comprehension of human mind.

All such experiences helped Justin to understand the areas where God was using him more visibly, as compared to the areas where he learnt just to wait upon Him. He was also learning to completely lean upon God.

THE FIRST GLANCE

THE BROCHURE WORK had picked up at a feverish pace; all the articles for the brochure were final and Justin and Sushmita were working on the layout of the same. Stealing the time from other essentials, they were devoting many hours to this work to meet the deadline. That morning, Sushmita reached early as usual to prepare some snacks for Justin and herself, as that would sustain them until the evening. Frequently, Justin would also have to go to the office of the lithographer, who was developing film of negative-screens in CMYK that were needed to make metal plates for colour printing.

When Justin reached the church office, Sushmita was standing in the small kitchen area preparing cold coffee and some kind of quick snack. Attired in a light grey belted sleeveless tunic she was expertly balancing herself on stiletto heels.

Her hair was tied up carelessly in a bun with a few strands of them dangling mischievously on her round face. Despite the absence of makeup, her face glowed with radiance. She had beautiful and very expressive eyes and when she smiled, one could see the sparkly row of pearly, white teeth. The snugly fitting tunic showed off the contours of her beautiful figure.

'What's happening to me?' Justin thought aloud, feeling disturbed by his own reaction. For quite some time, he had not reacted like this towards any other person of the fair sex. He was quite content with his marriage and, during the course of time, had strengthened himself against such feelings of lasciviousness. However, today, he repeatedly had an urge to steal a glance at Sushmita.

Together, they sat for coffee and light snack and in order to get himself out of this frame of mind, Justin finished his snacks quickly and left the small dining area. Sitting down at the coffee table that was in the office area, he picked up the stack of edited papers and started going through them. Soon, he realised that his mind was not with him and though he was intently looking at the papers, still he was not able to make anything out of them. Within a few minutes, Sushmita joined him at the table and sat opposite him. It was an effort on Justin's part to avoid looking at her. After some time, Sushmita got up from her chair, picked up some papers and came and knelt beside him, propping herself up with her arms resting on the table. Justin, seated on the chair, peered down at her, when his eyes caught sight of her breasts that were bared by the cloth of her tunic, which had folded forward, exposing her flesh to his sight. In his vulnerable state, that was the last thing Justin could have endured that day. Numbed, he did not know how long he held his gaze in that direction until he heard the nudging 'Hey' of Sushmita that snapped him out of his stupor.

'What happened?' she asked, with her eyebrows arched up and a puzzled expression in her eyes.

'N...nothing', stammered Justin, he could not take this anymore and, in a huff, stepped out of the office leaving behind a perplexed Sushmita.

Outside, the temperatures were soaring high and within a few minutes, he had to make a hasty retreat to the cool interior of the office.

Meanwhile, Sushmita had seated herself on the sofa and was sipping her cold coffee with a confused and sullen expression. Justin sat down quietly at an angle to her and tried to pull some papers out of the stack with the purpose of working on them when, suddenly, Sushmita swiftly slapped his hand, saying, 'Don't touch that'.

Now it was Justin's turn to be surprised by her action, 'What happened?'

'Why did you walk out of the room?'

'Just like that'.

'No, and you know it', her voice was emphatic.

'I was feeling overwhelmed by the heat'.

'Overwhelmed, yes you were overwhelmed, but not by the heat. You are overwhelmed by my presence', replied Sushmita in a matter of fact tone.

'Why would I be overwhelmed by you? You are here every day'.

'Are you scared of me?' Sushmita asked as if throwing a challenge at him.

'Why would I be scared of you, what are you inferring by all this?' Justin asked, now genuinely baffled by the turn of events.

Getting up from her chair, travelling those few steps with confidence, Sushmita came and sat down on the coffee table directly in front of Justin.

'Am I kissable?' she questioned, at which Justin nearly fell off his chair.

'I don't understand what are you getting at?' Justin said in an alarmed voice.

'A simple and straightforward question and I expect to hear a simple and straightforward answer from a man like you. Am I kissable?' Sushmita continued her query in a very assertive way. All this talk was taking a toll on Justin. He was fighting within himself, trying hard to suppress his base instincts that by now were trying to get the better of him.

'How would I know?' Justin said with a confused expression on his face.

Sushmita was now sitting so close to him that he could feel

the heat radiate from her body. Her face was close in a very titillating way; her lips, soft and parted.

'H-How would I know?' he stammered again in a whisper.

'Find out for yourself', Sushmita sounded as if from a distance.

Everything got blurred in the sight of Justin, except the beautiful face in front of him. Very softly, he leaned forward and put his lips very lightly on her beautiful lips; he stayed there for two or three seconds and then parted from them very gently. This was the first time Justin held her beauty so closely; with her eyes closed, she looked devastatingly beautiful. He noticed that her eyebrows curved up like the wings of an eagle, as if soaring in the sky. Her eyelashes turned upwards like the 'wave' of the tumultuous sea, a wave that races towards the shore, where, in the end, it curves up and back before it shatters into thousands of very fine droplets, each giving rise to its own rainbow. In between this sky and the sea, Justin could distinctly make out the blue veins on her closed eyelids branching out as if tributaries of a river.

Justin could not hold himself back any longer. He bent down once again and this time, softly put his lips on her closed eyelids as if to quench his thirst from those tributaries. Slowly, Sushmita raised her arms and put them around his neck. Justin gently responded by drawing her towards him with his arms around her waist, and again softly kissed her parted lips. There was no active response from her to his kiss and he was in the process of pulling himself away when she locked his lips down with her own, and they exchanged a long, drawn out, gentle kiss. When they parted, Justin held her face between his hands looking deep into her big eyes and covered it with sweet kisses. They held each other in that stance for a long time until Justin firmly pushed himself away from her. Breathing heavily now, they both sat down for some time trying to hold their composure. At last, they both opened their mouths stammering simultaneously, 'I love you'.

The weight of the moment was too much for either of them to bear, and as if in a trance, they departed to their homes. Justin could not understand his own actions and once at home, he tried to keep to himself, though with Pearl and the boys around, it was rather impossible. That night, Justin could not sleep properly. Lying on one side of the bed and facing the wall on the far end, he kept reliving those moments repeatedly.

The next day morning, he got ready with a new sense of excitement that made his body shiver a little. With the same hyped up feeling, he reached the church office only to find that it was still closed and Sushmita had not come as per her routine. He kept pacing up and down the office area. At the slightest noise from the street, he would peek out repeatedly by slightly parting the curtain on the window, only to drop it back with disappointment in his heart. Sushmita did not show up that day, and there was no way for Justin to make out the reason.

SPIRIT & FLESH

ASHOK, A MAN of few words and humble to the core, was a big-boned fellow. Justin would usually meet him twice a week: once in the Sunday church service and again during the mid-week prayer meeting. In these times, when it was unfashionable to put oil in one's hair, this man always had his set of coarse hair greased up. The same coarse hair made up the big mustache he kept. Armed with a leather bag with his Bible secured in it, he was a well-known person in these church cell meetings. With his head slightly tilted forward at an angle, his eyes beholding the person in front, he was always there to lend his ear to people with concern in their lives.

Within a few years into the full-time ministry, Justin laid hands on different people whose spiritual gifts became evident to the church. Ashok was one of them—a man of fasting and prayer, a proverbial prayer warrior. He was the man who, with a few other dedicated members, could go down on their knees and pray for others.

That particular Sunday morning, the church was full. Many new people from surrounding areas were there on their maiden visit to the church. The church had a good worship team that had young people accompanied by their musical instruments. The Sunday worship started with gusto and very soon, the whole congregation was completely engrossed in the worship.

There were times when someone from the congregation would bring forth a word of wisdom for the edification of the body of Christ. During the time of worship, when Justin made an altar call, many people came and assembled near the pulpit. Justin prompted Ashok and other minister to lay their hands and pray for the people according to their needs. Pearl was praying in the area where more women had gathered for prayer when, suddenly, a young woman in her mid-twenties started to make strange sounds like a low growl. Justin, who was prayerfully overseeing the scene, quietly prompted Ashok to go over and pray for that woman. At the very first step that Ashok took in the direction of the woman, her growls became more pronounced and the people who had brought her to the service found it difficult to contain her violent movements. Her flailing arms struck a few members in the vicinity and quickly, everyone cleared the area around her.

The worship team continued to play their instruments and the worship went on. For many in the church, this was not the first experience; however, a few faint-hearted people and those who had never witnessed any such thing receded to the far end of the hall. By now, the woman had a disheveled appearance and was growling and swinging her arms and as Justin and Ashok approached her, she looked threateningly at them through her bloodshot eyes. The standoff continued for a minute or two when, in a calm and composed voice, Ashok rebuked the evil spirit to depart. There was shudder and tearing-off as if something was violently leaving the woman. After a few minutes of silence, the woman showed signs of extreme exhaustion and stumbled on her feet though the ushers moved quickly to support and make her to sit on a chair.

Slowly, the worship started again and the service continued.

That Sunday proved to be a very long and eventful day and by the time Justin had done meeting the congregants, Sushmita had already left the church.

It was late in the evening when Justin reached home with his family. The boys needed to go to school the next day so in spite their hyperactive stance they were dismissed for the night.

Once in their room, Pearl and Justin discussed with excitement the happenings of the day; the church was growing and so were various church ministries. They talked about the need to open another church branch in West Delhi for which Ashok was the unanimous choice as a minister.

STRUGGLE BETWEEN FLESH & BLOOD

THAT MONDAY MORNING, Justin felt the urgency with which the brochure work needed to be taken up, as there were very few days left before all the print material needed to be handed over to the offset printer. After Pearl and the boys had left, Justin got ready and left for the church office. Once there, he noticed that Sushmita had not come. He felt uneasy about this, as until then, she had never showed a casual attitude towards her responsibilities. While opening the office, he was thinking of reasons that could have kept Sushmita from coming that morning. In fact, that past Sunday also he did not get a chance to meet her after the church service. Justin started to wonder as to why his thoughts were constantly focusing on Sushmita. Was it because of the pressure of the work, or was he missing her in a personal way?

Firmly suppressing any such feelings, he prepared himself to get down with the work. An hour passed as Justin tried to attend to several important aspects of the brochure, when he heard the gate open and footsteps approaching. The door opened and his heart nearly skipped a beat. Followed by her uncle, Sushmita was walking through the doorway. Justin greeted both of them with enthusiasm.

Sushmita immediately proceeded to the kitchen while her uncle settled with Justin in the office area.

'Brother, today Sushmita wanted me to come and meet you', said her uncle looking straight in his eyes.

'Tell me, brother', was Justin's short reply; at the same time, he threw a glance towards Sushmita who, after starting the coffee machine, was standing in the doorway. There was no expression on her face, which worried Justin as he was still trying to figure out the intent behind her uncle's statement.

'I am sorry. Yesterday, we all had to leave immediately after the church service as we needed to be at the train station to receive my brother who was coming from Jhansi'.

'Oh! No problem, brother'.

Standing at the doorway of the kitchen with coffee mugs in her hand, Sushmita had a mischievous smile on her face. Looking towards her, Justin asked, 'And why did you not come the other day? The brochure work is lagging behind schedule'.

'Well I just wanted you to know how important I am for your work and if I miss one day, the work suffers', she said with the same mischievous look. Her uncle, picking up on the joke, gave a hearty laugh. They all had coffee and her uncle finding the morning newspaper, engaged himself with the latest news.

Sushmita and Justin started with the brochure work that demanded their undivided attention. Justin was working perfectly fine but his mind was multitasking—editing the various articles for the brochure yet thinking about Sushmita, who was looking gorgeous.

It seemed she had taken extra care to do her makeup that day. It accentuated some of her features that, in fact, made her look ravishing. Well, at least to Justin. Wearing big, circular hoops in her ears and a pearl necklace around her neck with matching bracelets, she was a beautiful, young woman with a mind of her own. Attired in a skirt and a spaghetti-strap top, with a small sleeveless jacket casually thrown over it, she completed her beauty statement with her signature stilettos, and her looks with a purpose … to kill!

They kept working for quite some time while her uncle kept himself busy with the newspaper. At last, bearing no more, Sushmita looked at her uncle and reminded him that he was to go to work.

'Ah yes! I was reading some interesting article and got carried away. Well, I should leave immediately, take care both of you', and within five minutes, he was gone.

Justin and Sushmita kept looking at each other for quite some time. Except for the whirling sound made by the fan of the air-cooler, everything was quiet. It seemed they both could hear each other's heartbeats.

'I missed you yesterday'. Justin spoke after a long pause.

'I don't know what has happened to me; I keep thinking about you the way I should not. It is not proper, but it seems I do not have any control on my thoughts'.

'I also have been very restless these days', Sushmita said. 'It seems I want you around me all the time. I also know that it is not proper, for you are a married man but…. Maybe we should give way to our inner feelings, not fight them, and this may pass after sometime'.

Justin being more mature and a preacher of the Word knew perfectly well that they should not give-in to their feelings. He even wanted to say that aloud but could not muster the courage to speak the truth. His spirit was prompting him to speak out and take charge of the situation in the righteous way but his flesh, which was yearning the closeness of Sushmita, was guiding him otherwise. It wanted to concur with what she had just said that they should let their feelings take hold of the situation and it will pass with time. Justin's inner self on the other hand was telling him 'NO', if they give-in even once, they would never be able to come out of it.

With brochure material all around, they sat close to each other trying to suppress the desires of their flesh and start the work, but the closeness of their bodies was generating such heat that it slowly started to cloud their thinking. Sushmita's cheeks were glowing. The perfume that she was wearing created an aura of its own, numbing their senses and transporting them in a world where the awareness for their bodies was diminishing all other virtues. Soon, they found themselves holding each other with a closeness that was making everything in the room look fuzzy, though they were still trying hard in their own ways to ward off the carnal desire to melt into each other's arms. All of a sudden, the telephone bell rang, shattering the enticing silence in the atmosphere. It was a call from the office of the lithographer who said that in an hour he would drop by the church office, with the proof of the material readied for print.

Suddenly, it dawned upon them that they would soon lose this solitude. Within those moments, Justin experienced a fierce battle of the spirit and flesh rage within himself. The spirit was telling him in no uncertain words that *this* was the moment to let go off Sushmita while his flesh craved for her nearness and his mind wanted to drown in her dreamy eyes this *one time* only, after which he would not burn for her with lust.

This one time only, blurred his thinking completely and with a mute cry, Justin tore off the protective covering of his spirit to fall prey to his own carnal desires.

With a force so great as if their very life depended upon it, they came together in a tight embrace, ravishing each other with kisses that were no more gentle, but intense and demanding. Sushmita's billowy lips had turned red by his kisses. The spaghetti straps of her top fell off by themselves, and made bare her slender shoulders. Like a man, as if possessed, he pressed his lips on them, planting kisses everywhere on the flesh that he beheld from her face to her bare shoulders. She, in turn, was panting heavily, her breath feeling like fire on his face. Lost in each other, they would not have noted the presence of the man from the lithographer's office bringing the proof if not for the outer gate in the front yard, which made a creaky sound every time someone opened it. The two realised they were about to be discovered. Sushmita quickly disappeared in the kitchen area to straighten her disheveled dress and become presentable. Justin, on the other hand, immediately took quick steps towards the mirror on the wall to pat down his hair, when he noticed lipstick marks on his face. He had just enough time to rub them off with his handkerchief when the gentleman opened the office door and stepped in. 'Phew', escaped Justin's suppressed sigh of relief. His heart was pounding so hard that he feared that others could hear it loud and clear. His feet were trembling and he found it difficult to keep his balance. His ears felt as if they were on fire and must have turned red out of anxiety. Soon, Sushmita came out of the kitchen carrying a glass of water and Justin noticed that her composure was far better than his own was.

The man from the lithographer left after finishing his business, and soon Sushmita too, left for work. Left alone, Justin sat down on the sofa, and it was then that the happenings of the last few hours dawned upon him. His emotions swayed from excitement to remorse. Thinking about his tryst with Sushmita, the hairs on the nape of his neck stood on end but, on the other hand, regret-wallowing deep inside his heart.

As if in a flash, he went through all the bountiful goodness of God that he had experienced since he entered the full-time ministry versus today's actions wherein he sure would have failed Him miserably. Filled with such emotions, he went home. The boys were there and the younger one was ready, as usual, to share with him his adventures at school. However, not getting a very enthusiastic response from Justin, the younger one went away complaining to his grandmother.

In the night, when everyone had gone to sleep, Justin sat down to study his Bible as it was Thursday night and he had to preach in the Sunday church service. However, he could not understand anything from the Bible. There were no revelations coming his way, nor any of his earlier thoughts that he had noted down in his diary made any sense to him. He closed the Bible and started to pray but he could not feel the excitement in his spirit; he got scared of the void that he was feeling. Has God left him, and would he not be able to preach in the upcoming meetings? Greatly disturbed with such thoughts he went to bed in the wee hours of the morning. By the time he woke up, Pearl and the boys had left for their respective vocations.

CONVENTION

OR THE NEXT two days, Justin sat down with the Bible and continued in his meditation. For a long time, he just could not get any thoughts for the upcoming meetings to the extent that he was getting distressed, when ultimately, in the middle of the night, the Word that he was reading quickened his spirit and he started to feel comfortable.

The Sunday church service went on very nicely and the thoughts shared by Justin from the Bible blessed everyone. Once home from the church, the boys became busy preparing for school the next day, while Pearl and Justin sat down in their bedroom discussing the church meetings. All of a sudden, Pearl asked if everything was all right with Sushmita, as she was not looking her usual self in the church. Justin expressed his ignorance towards anything unusual in the matter. She continued saying that she noticed Sushmita looking at him intently during the church service. He became cautious on hearing that statement but responded with the shrug of his shoulders and tried to change the subject. Justin did not want Pearl to dwell further on the subject because he knew his face might give him away. However, her observation troubled and surprised him. He thought to himself, *what am I getting into?*

That night, he seriously prayed for himself so that he may not fall into this temptation again. He loved his God, he loved the ministry, he loved his wife, he loved his family, and he did not want to jeopardise any of it. Justin's commitments to all were genuine and sincere.

The next morning, before going to the church office, he called James, a church member who, as per Justin's knowledge, was free on that Monday morning and asked him if he could devote some time to the brochure work, as the date was drawing closer. James expressed his willingness, so Justin picked him up on the way to the church office. Once at the office, they immediately got down with the brochure work. After nearly an hour, Sushmita arrived, and she was surprised to see James there. When told that James would help them with the work that day, she indirectly expressed her displeasure with the idea by not communicating with Justin. All his queries about the work faced a stonewall. That day, they were able to accomplish quite a lot with the brochure work but Sushmita kept her stance of not speaking, while at the same time chatted up James to Justin's chagrin. In the evening, James needed to attend to some work so he left an hour before the usual time Sushmita and Justin would leave otherwise.

Once James had left, it took lot of coaxing on Justin's part to make Sushmita talk to him. The first thing that she asked was the reason he brought James to the office without giving her a heads-up. However, without waiting for his answer, she continued to say that Pearl was being nosy about her the other day. Now it was Justin's turn to be surprised.

'What was that about Pearl being pushy with you?' Justin asked with concern in his voice.

'Well, yesterday after the church, Pearl came up to me and asked if I was okay. When I said that everything was fine, she persisted and asked if I wanted to say something to the Pastor that is you'.

'So what did you tell her?'

'I said that yes, I need to see the pastor, to which she asked if she could be of some help instead. Now does she have a problem with that? Why should she have a problem if I am looking at you? Everyone looks at the pastor, right?' was the question thrown directly at Justin.

'Ah I see...' was the small reply that was cut short by the sound of Sushmita's stomping feet.

All of a sudden, everything became clear to Justin—the undercurrents that brought this turbulence between the two women, Pearl's sarcastic comments, Sushmita's aggressive posture, and everything in between. It was something to be alarmed about—there was problem brewing and it was getting serious.

Sushmita's voice interrupted his thoughts, 'You didn't tell me why you had to bring James with you this morning'.

Justin was never a quick-witted person. Whether this attribute was good or bad, this was not the time to think about it. At her insistence, he truthfully answered saying that the other day, Pearl *did* tell him about her observation that Sushmita was looking at him intently. He explained that in order to quell such thoughts—'ones' that Pearl was *already* entertaining—he thought it proper to bring James along with him.

In fact, Justin's statement infuriated Sushmita even more and in a second, she swooped and sat down next to him. Taking his face in her hands, she asked him, 'Do you love me?' Justin, who just yesterday was seriously thinking of having a talk with Sushmita and put his inordinate affections for her behind him, again found himself looking into those light brown eyes that had bewitched him before.

He truly loved God and wanted to serve Him with sincerity. At home, he had firmly decided to tell Sushmita what they were getting into was inappropriate—a sin, in fact—and that they needed to keep their relationship pure, but now looking into her eyes, with her sitting so close to him, his flesh and mind were telling him not to say anything of those. Instead, her closeness made him excited all over again. He could feel his body responding wildly with just the thought of holding her in his arms. He had kissed those beautiful lips before and they were there for him to savour once again. Her luscious figure was filling his imagination with thoughts of unspeakable pleasures. His trichotomous being was losing control and his dichotomous self was gaining advantage. A tremendous struggle raged between his spirit and flesh. His thoughts from the other night—his commitment to God, his commitment to Pearl, the thoughts about his sons— were getting clouded, and a strong desire to savour the moment was overpowering Justin. Unable to contain the desires of his flesh any longer, with a strong pull of his arms he scooped her up unto his lap; his lips pressing hard against hers. For a few moments, she went limp in his arms by the suddenness of his reaction, but then her lips responded to his onslaught with an urgency that made them both go dizzy in the head. Each gasp for breath was filled with proclamations of love. She dug her teeth deep in his shoulders and her nails in his back while his hands explored the soft roundness of her bosom, the apex of which had become taut by the touch of his fingers. Swooning with ecstasy, soon they found themselves bringing each other to 'pleasures' without the act of consummation. After the rush of euphoria was over, they held each other very intimately, looking dreamily in one another's eyes. Not wanting the blissful moments to pass, they kept on confessing their love for one another, exchanging small kisses all the while.

SAMANTHA SOLOMON

S HE WAS AN avid fan of Justin as a preacher. Though an elder in her own Main Line church, she would always find time to attend Justin's church meetings. Following the heritage of a family that devoted itself to impart education in the city of Delhi, Samantha Solomon, a high school teacher, was a well-respected figure. Her elderly mother, an educationist of the years of yore, would drop by unannounced in the church office and talk at length with Justin on biblical subjects.

One fine morning, Samantha received a call from one of her close relatives that her uncle Mr. Patrick who had been hospitalised repeatedly in the past was again taken ill and he wanted to see her before proceeding to the hospital. She called Justin and requested him to come along with her in the evening to pray for her uncle. Justin never took such occasions lightly and as such in the evening he, along with Pearl, reached Samantha Solomon's house. From there, they traveled in her car to go to her uncle's place, which was near the famous *Kutab Minar* of Delhi. As soon as they entered the room where her uncle was lying on the bed, Justin felt some kind of heaviness in his heart. There was another person present in the room—the pastor of Samantha's church, of which she was officially the member. Samantha felt a bit uneasy for the sake of Justin but soon his conduct made her feel comfortable. By now, Justin had learnt the art of making himself—and others—comfortable in situations like this when pastors from Main Line churches were also present. Pastor Simon, a small-statured person with a moustache styled after Charlie Chaplin, acknowledged Justin and Pearl's presence with the nod of his head. Then, with a very pleased expression on his face, he continued the conversation that he was having with Samantha's uncle. Soon, Mr. Patrick handed over a few signed checks to Pastor Simon and said that the amount was a donation from him to the church. In spite of the seriousness of the situation, Justin could not ignore the twinkle in Pastor Simon's eyes, that he felt directed at him. Soon thereafter, Pastor Simon said a prayer in all its grandiloquence and left the place.

All along, Justin was feeling the heaviness in his heart about this man whom he was meeting for the first time. Mr. Patrick, the elderly man whose gray hair gave him the respectability of age, was lying down on his bed in this very well furnished room. Samantha introduced him to Justin and Pearl as a very accomplished man—a person of great standing in church and the society at large, and that he had a very generous heart. The last attribute needed no mention as Justin and Pearl had just witnessed it.

Justin continued to feel very uncomfortable in his spirit and after some time, gathering great courage, he asked Samantha and others of the family to leave the room as he wanted to be alone with the gentleman. At their departure, he opened up his Bible reading a few passages from it and exhorting Mr. Patrick to seek forgiveness for his sins and ask for the Lord's mercy. Justin told him that, in the presence of God, our righteousness is but like rags and we all need to approach him with a broken spirit and a contrite heart. Most unexpectedly, and to the amazement of Justin and Pearl, the elderly man started to cry with tears slowly welling up in his eyes. He stretched forth his hand to hold Justin's and soon started to sob uncontrollably. Justin let him pour out his heart in silence in front of God and then after some time, again led him in prayer.

On the way back, Samantha asked Justin about the happenings inside the room and he told her that her uncle needed to give and to receive. He needed to give his heart to God with all humility and in return, receive his salvation; and Justin believed that is exactly what happened in that room.

After three days, Samantha called Justin to tell that her uncle passed away the other morning, and that he was very peaceful and even told his family members that he was ready to leave.

'Amen', said Justin. He decided to attend the funeral of her uncle that was to take place that afternoon at a cemetery in Khan Market.

Envy & Cemetery!

IN THE CITY of Delhi, Pastors representing churches of different denominations at times get thrown together by circumstances and attend funerals of deceased Christians who were well known in the community. Apart from the grief of the families and the consolation offered by all and sundry during such funerals, there was also a 'hidden element' during such a solemn time: an 'element' of competition between the pastors from different churches. It happened at the funeral of deceased Mr. Patrick too. Justin found that although this spirit of rivalry was hidden from the eyes of the people who had come to attend the funeral, it was still ever-present amongst the clergy in attendance. The spirit of envy in a cemetery may sound 'unreal' but that is exactly what Justin had experienced on many such occasions. It used to become a testing ground for pastors—their influence, their scriptural knowledge, how well they could recite scriptures without referring to any written text, and their capability to lead the procession by singing time-tested hymns, masterfully modulating their vocal chords to change notes from bass to tenor. They would say prayers, interwoven with long passages from the scriptures, with the show of emotions that were compounded with resonating deep-throated voices, the cry of which seemed to reach the heavens itself. How many followers each clergy had on the site, how many people attending the funeral paid them their respect—all such things added to the respectability of the attending pastors.

Justin reached the funeral ground wearing his black jacket with his small reference notebook kept in the inside pocket. In due course, the funeral entourage arrived and the accompanying people disembarked from their vehicles. Pastor Simon stepped out from the lead car wearing a white, double-breasted cassock complete with an overlay purple tapestry stole and strode purposefully to take his place at the head of the procession. Various pastors from other Main Line churches quickly joined him. This array of church ministers wearing their white or black cassocks and priestly robes of various hues, reciting lessons from the scripture at the top of their voices with a heavy accent, led the procession to the place where the freshly dug grave was prepared.

Justin, by his experience, had known that making a place in the hearts of people was easy but gaining acknowledgment from a pastor belonging to another denomination was near impossible. By now, he had learnt to deal with such situations and kept his pace behind the leading band of the pastors. He was relieved when, after a while, Samantha and some other family members of the deceased joined him on the way. At the site of the freshly dug grave, when the people accompanying the procession had taken their places, Pastor Simon started to speak and requested the other pastors to assist him in the burial ceremony—in the process completely, purposefully, and successfully ignoring Justin. It was at this moment that the brother of the deceased quickly scribbled something on a small piece of paper and passed it on to Pastor Simon, who had just opened his Bible to start the burial ceremony. While looking at the contents of the note, his countenance changed but quickly overcoming it, he announced that the memorial service for the Late Mr. Patrick was to take place the week after in Pastor Simon's church and the family desired Mr. Justin to bring forth the Word of God on that day. He never liked addressing Justin as 'Pastor' but rather took pleasure in addressing him as Mr. Justin. In spite of being the leader of a very big church Pastor Simon was beset with some kind of insecurity and Justin knew that he was the last person to like the idea of him speaking at the memorial service—and that, too, in his own church. However, by God's grace, people appreciated the way Justin expounded the Word from the Bible, in contrast to many pastors of Main Line churches, and Justin was thankful to God for this anointing.

After the burial service, Justin rushed back to the church office, as the brochure work needed his attention. In addition, he also needed to take care of a few arrangements for the upcoming convention in the city of Agra.

FOOD EATEN IN SECRET

THE FIFTH ANNIVERSARY celebration of the church proved to be very successful and many people attended the weekend meetings. The brochure was not only received as a very good piece of publication but also gave a great impetus to the church work. Justin attributed a lot of credit to Sushmita for working on the brochure though Pearl did not appreciate it and once at home, she was mildly vocal about it in front of him. Justin started to notice clear negative vibes that had started to build between Pearl and Sushmita, which concerned him. However, to his amazement, it also gave him a feeling of thrill that was amusing in itself. The more Pearl expressed her displeasure, the more Justin got attracted to Sushmita, which of course was absolutely no excuse for him to do what he was doing. On the contrary, he found himself defending his actions. Justin started contemplating the biblical character of King David and Bathsheba's relationship in a different way to justify his own wayward steps.

After the brochure work, Justin and Sushmita found it difficult to meet each other under any pretext, so they had to resort to talking over the phone. This was not easy because there were always chances that someone from the family may pick up the phone on the other side. They tried solving this by alerting each other by first, giving a short blank call and then making the actual call. One day, however, over casual talks, the two families exchanged notes of increase in prank calls to their respective places, making Sushmita and Justin uncomfortable because the coincidence was too much to be dismissed.

By now, Mr. & Mrs. Goodwin and Brother Eric had also noted the extraordinary, though subtle, interaction that Justin and Sushmita displayed, and Mr. Goodwin had even commented indirectly on the subject in the hearing of the two.

The preparations for the Agra convention were in full swing when suddenly Mrs. Goodwin fell sick. This was a problematic situation. Sushmita could only go to the convention if Mrs. Goodwin recovered well in time, because the Goodwins had requested Sushmita to stay back and look after her. Sushmita and Justin found themselves cornered as no argument against this *humanitarian* cause could be justified.

A gloom descended upon the two as they realised that they would not be able to enjoy each other's company during the days of the convention. Talking over the phone also would not be feasible as it would not be easy for Justin to leave the convention venue to go looking for the pay phone. Both were crestfallen but did not have a say in the matter for fear of being looked at suspiciously by all. On Tuesday evening, to the surprise of everyone, Sushmita and the Goodwins were present at the home fellowship meeting. Mrs. Goodwin, though still very weak from her sickness, seemed to be on the road to recovery.

After the meeting, stealthily, Sushmita passed a note to Justin, which he quickly put away in his pocket. Then, excusing himself with the pretext of using the restroom, he hurried to the confines of this only place of 'solitude'. Once inside, he quietly took out the note, and jumped with joy like a teenager when he read the words, 'I am coming to the convention'. He took great care to tear up the small piece of paper and flush it down the toilet.

Once outside, while mingling with the people, Justin made it a point to keep away from Sushmita, but at each glance that they exchanged, there was joy unspeakable in their eyes.

The journey to Agra needed to start at dusk on that Friday so that they could reach the convention venue by late night. The meeting point was the church office where everyone was to assemble by seven in the evening.

After taking leave from Pearl and the boys, Justin reached the church office much before everyone else. His heart was all excited about the prospect of being with Sushmita in those three days starting with the car journey, which itself would be more than four hours. Sushmita, along with the Goodwins, was the next to arrive, followed by Brother Eric. Lately, Justin observed that whenever he and Sushmita were in close vicinity, it attracted amused looks from Brother Eric, which both cautioned and irritated Justin at the same time. Nonetheless, putting aside all such thoughts, Sushmita and Justin continued to exchange glances beyond the customary greetings.

There was a small convoy of three cars, which had fourteen people in all. Of them, three were to share the ride with Justin in his car. The permutation and combinations could have been numerous but, somehow, without raising any red flags, Justin managed to get Sushmita to travel in his car with two more church members who were in their mid-thirties. The car driven by Sushmita's uncle had his wife, Brother Eric, and two others sharing the ride.

With her shoulder length hair flowing loosely, Sushmita was attired casually in jeans and a short top that exposed her midriff to the sight. She had a well-toned, flat belly with contours just at the right places. Sushmita did not have those rippling six-pack muscles, which in Justin's opinion were a manly attribute but instead had a soft, well-toned belly. Her short top left her navel uncovered, which presented such a mysterious look; hidden behind its own formation from where her belly with its fleshy contours sprouted, as if it was the bud of a lily from where its petals spread out rising slightly above before flattening smoothly. When she walked towards Justin in the fading golden light of the setting sun, the contours of her abdomen moved very slightly in a rhythm of their own, as if giving rise to a sensual song. Mentally, Justin was taking care of a few last minute arrangements for the journey; however, his heart and his roving eyes were still stuck at the 'nucleus', the belly button of Sushmita that showed every now and then with each movement. Oh, how he wished to peek inside that nucleus and the secrets it held! It seemed he needed to go down on the knees to bring his eyes at the level of this newfound nucleus of 'his' universe, gently spreading the soft flesh around it with both his hands to behold the secrets of treasures hidden therein. How Justin wanted to liven up his fantasy right then but alas, it was not to be so! In fact, right at that time, some more people who were a part of the entourage arrived, thus, jolting him out of his silly musings. Justin realised how preoccupied he was with thoughts of Sushmita.

Within the next quarter of an hour, everyone arrived and soon they hit the road. By the time, they were out of the city boundaries and onto the highway, darkness had spread its wings. Justin and the rest of the three were having lively conversation when Sushmita expressed her desire to stretch her legs and take a nap. To the delight of Justin and Sushmita, the two gentlemen seated on the rear seat suggested that she should stretch on the front seat itself and take a nap. *Andhe ko kya chahiye, do ankhen*, goes the saying in Hindi (what does a blind man need, two eyes). Sushmita immediately grabbed the idea and pulling up her shawl, curled up in the front seat of the car with her head nearly in Justin's lap, who was driving. The two men sitting in the rear seat of the car softly continued their conversation on some topic of intellectual interest, whereas Justin remained preoccupied with the fantasy of the nucleus, the beauty of which he had seen in the glimmer of the fading sunlight.

Suddenly, Justin realised that the owner of the precious jewel was in fact lying next to him in the car. Slowly and cautiously, he let his left hand slide towards the object of his desire. Once there, with great tenderness, his fingers touched it. The body lying next to him shivered and her hands slowly but firmly clutched him around the leg. At every touch, she would quiver and her whole body would become taut. For a long time he caressed her belly, with his fingers taking turns in stroking her navel, sometimes trying to spread it with two fingers and trying to pry in-between with the third.

All of a sudden, in the dark interior of the car, which got illuminated occasionally by the lights of the passing vehicles, Justin felt Sushmita's hands working up themselves around his lower midriff. He became taut because of the elements of fear and excitement that were working simultaneously upon him. Fear, because they could be chanced upon by the two gentlemen sitting just a few feet behind on the rear seat of the car and excitement, because Sushmita and him were indulging in the 'forbidden' right under the very nose of those two gentlemen.

They were risking everything that they had. Justin was particularly putting everything at stake, but still, the thrill of the forbidden had started to excite him every time he was close to Sushmita. That day also, was no different, it had become a game for them, a dangerous game, which they just could not resist to play.

As their forays into the flesh progressed so did the speed of the car. Driving with one hand, braving the onslaught of the glare created by the oncoming vehicles with their high beams, Justin by then was driving between 80 and 90 kmph on that rough highway, which was hardly 20 to 25 feet wide and catered from bullock cart to the heavily laden trucks. The two church members sitting on the rear seat and oblivious of the happenings trusted Justin in every way, his biblical knowledge and his driving skills too. At last, all the three climaxed together, the car with its speed touching 90 kmph; and Sushmita and Justin in their pursuit of fleshly pleasures.

'Brother, you are a very good driver', said one of the men sitting in the rear seat.

'Thank you', said Justin.

PROPINQUITY

THE PROPINQUITY THAT Sushmita had gained with her Pastor Justin was becoming a matter of concern for Justin's wife, Pearl. However, she did not allow her emotion to betray her, though for a discerning observer, there was a hint of perpetual sadness in her eyes. This situation had unsettled her from the inside, though outwardly she bravely tried to keep self-composed. It would be too much of a humiliation for her to share her grief with others; she was too proud of her married life. From the time she married Justin, she had never shared anything negative about themselves even with her parents or other siblings. Did she miss her father? 'Yes', 'maybe'. Earlier she could go to her father with all her problems and concerns but now she felt so lonely. Justin had replaced her father so completely in her life that, for the first time, she felt that she had no one to turn to. The only thing that kept her from drowning in this sea of sorrow, that was engulfing her so completely, was her prayer life. Pearl's prayer ministry had brought solace and comfort to many in the church, but it seemed as if in spite of her fervently seeking God's intervention in her own life, the prayers were not answered.

Few members of the church also started feeling an undercurrent between Justin and Sushmita, but none had the heart to acknowledge that something of this nature was happening and thus gather the courage to take up the matter with Justin, their

Pastor. Many from other sister churches including Brother Eric may have preached to the congregants in Justin's church, but as most were spiritually born of Justin, he was a fatherly figure and a mentor to them. Such subjects are taboo and not discussed. People just try to wish them away as a bad dream.

Meanwhile, Justin was also not oblivious of the prying eyes of a few of the church members, constantly following him whenever Sushmita was in vicinity. He had a strong feeling that others may have also noticed Pearl's withdrawn expression and how, after the church service, she would only devote her time with the people who wanted her to pray for their concerns. That was not unusual; the unusual was that now this was the only activity she participated in. Sometimes, while praying for others and fervently interceding with God on behalf of them, Justin occasionally felt that Pearl's own grief reflected in the prayers by way of outbursts. On such occasions, frightened to face Pearl, Sushmita would make a hasty retreat.

When alone in their stolen moments, Sushmita and Justin started discussing with concern the new developments in their lives. The guilt of committing sin in the sight of God and wronging so many people would often overwhelm them. Many-a-times, they tried hard to stay away from each other, but to no avail as it always proved to be counterproductive. Often, such concerns were instrumental in drawing them closer with such intensity that they would fall into each other's arms with renewed vigour. By then, they had realised that their relationship had crossed the 'infatuation' phase and they were completely and sincerely dedicated to each other with commitments exchanged for a lifetime. Justin and Sushmita loved each other for what they were. They were attracted to each other due to their varied interests; their literary interests glued them together. Justin loved her youthfulness, straightforward and outgoing nature, whereas Sushmita loved his sobriety, calm and reserved nature. When in each other's company, they would lose all concept of time. Their relationship did not hinge any more on immediate gratification but had developed deeper roots in their lives.

Each waking moment, they would think about each other. At the first opportunity, they would call and talk endlessly over the phone and every time they were close, they would just melt in each other's arms. In spite of all the odds, Justin and Sushmita were convinced that they were meant to be together. Every now and then, and even in absentia, they would feel the strong surge of loving emotions that would make their hearts ache for each other.

Being a pastor, Justin always felt a strong tug at his heart to repent and reform his ways; however, during every such thought, he would also convince himself that God was not angry with him and his relationship with God was intact, for every time he rose to deliver a sermon from the pulpit, it would bless everyone.

There is no ambiguity in the fact that one can maintain a relationship with God by being nowhere else but in His kingdom; that is, by maintaining the boundaries as set in the Bible for social behavior! Yet many, like Justin, carry on their self-will on the sly and live in denial, strangely enough all their lives!

Man forgets that he is simply an instrument for God to carry out His desires and plan and only His sovereign-self decides how far He would go to use the mortal for His purpose.

Justin's continued efficacious preaching from the Bible was one such example. In fact, God tarries for long.

The Bible says, '…Yet God does not take away a life; but He devises means, so that His banished ones are not expelled from Him.' (2 Samuel 14: 14)

In the Old Testament, a reference is made of King Saul of Israel where he was disobedient to God's specific command. Thereafter, the pronouncement came that Saul's kingdom will not last forever. However, the following chapters tell in detail that in spite of the decree, Saul's sovereignty over the kingdom of Israel continued for a long period of time, and wherever he went he was successful. Such references pacified Justin about his ministry, and drawing comparison would rationalise that God was still blessing his pastoral ministry.

The scripture says,

'Because the sentence against an evil work is not executed speedily, therefore the heart of the sons of men is fully set in them to do evil.' (Ecclesiastes Ch. 8: 11)

Preaching the Word of God was the most important thing in Justin's life without which, he would feel incomplete, lost, wasted. However, conflicting thoughts were constantly on the rise in his heart and that was not a good sign for his ministry.

In Justin's life, it was not a question of relativeness, as he made out to his own benefit, because God's word does not stand on some law of relativity—it has its own authority, it stands alone. God's Word is *crystal* clear, though people in Justin's shoes always play with the Word to suit their own motives. An elderly minister from one of the sister churches would always tell Justin the same and sometimes, even gather courage to tell Justin that he was treading a wrong path. However, Justin would dislodge him by pointing to various examples from the Old Testament of various characters that were weak towards the fair sex. The poor minister would just shake his head and not say anything further. Standing himself on slippery ground, Justin would momentarily take pride in that; he had aptly dealt with the probing senior.

Justin would preach on all the subjects from the Bible and his church members were growing deeper in the understanding of the Word of God; they were a very prayerful lot and doers of the Word. Justin noticed that he freely and effectively preached from the Bible but never broached upon the subject of sexual immorality, his own weak point.

STRATEGISING THE EXIT

NO ONE WOULD believe it. All the wise would dispute it, but the fact remained that the most important thing in Justin's life was church ministry. Ultimately, unable to counter the ever-rising turmoil within them, Justin and Sushmita seriously started thinking of getting away from the scene in order to bring least harm to the church. However, in all this, they were ignoring the fact that instead of adopting an exit strategy, they should try much harder to pull apart from each other and save all that mattered—the ministry, their families, children and their own lives.

The scripture says,

'Can a man take fire to his bosom, and his clothes not be burned?' (Proverbs 6: 27)

One thing was slowly becoming clear to both of them—by now, quite a few people in the church were throwing curious glances towards them. Justin and Sushmita could feel the unspoken disapproval that was gathering momentum.

This mild opposition, coupled with fear of being caught, brings about two things—either it scares you away or it fans the passions more. In the life of Justin and Sushmita, it caused the increase of adrenaline activity that activates the 'fight or flight' response system in the body. For these two lovebirds, it produced a strange mix of 'fight or flight' response, and fanned the passions to such an extent that, though fearing being caught, one still pursues the forbidden pleasures and does not fear the consequences. Repeat offences not only make a person bold in his or her unethical behavior, but also hasten steps towards destruction. Justin and Sushmita were always fearful about the 'what if' situations but were also getting bold by each passing day to experiment with more of 'what ifs'. They were concerned about the negative impact it would bring on the church members but at the same time had gone beyond the fear to fall. They never wanted to hurt anyone—noble thoughts—yet their actions brought about hurt to all and sundry. Thoughts—however noble they may be, if not backed by the strength of character to control the urge towards fulfillment of carnal desires would fall in the ambit of what the writer of the proverbs aptly describes, *'Stolen waters are sweet, and bread eaten in secret is pleasant' (Proverbs 9: 17).* The word 'stolen' robs the water and bread of their nature of imparting life, instead; the writers says further in the proverbs, it brings about death.

All these happenings also prompted Sushmita to give a deeper thought as to where their lives were heading in relation to the real world and how long they could carry on like this on the sly. She started giving serious thought about the need for her to settle down in life as Justin, for all practical purposes, was socially well entrenched in life sans her. Sushmita also started becoming more possessive about Justin and could no longer stand the 'Pastor couple' eating together from the same platter on social occasions. She always had a friendly say in the matters pertaining to Justin's family but now her proxy input in much of Justin's family matters became more pronounced.

Pearl was aware of these moves and to counter Sushmita's forays into her domain, she started to take more charge of the family matters and became more assertive towards Justin. Justin saw a fierce rivalry started to lift its ugly head between the two women in relation to him. In the beginning, it became very demanding upon him but then slowly to his amazement he started to enjoy the adulation, which came his way from the two women.

As the prying eyes following Justin and Sushmita became more intense, so did the fire and the desperation against all odds heightened between them. The intensity of this fire, in a way, welded them together more intensely and their commitment to each other against all wisdom kept growing stronger. They were up and against all their well-wishers, against all good counsel, and slowly but surely, their entities started to merge with each other against anything good that they ever had in them.

It was true! They were not able to handle their misplaced passion, which was now becoming the force driving them to the unknown territories of the world of darkness. They were losing hold of wisdom, and instead, dictates of passion started to control their lives.

Just after the inception of the church work, Brother Eric had introduced Pastor Bose to the congregation of Delhi. In one of his messages, he had pierced the heart of the whole congregation. Many, including Justin, made commitment to follow God's Word in their lives. The key verses said thus:

> *'Behold, I set before you today a blessing and a curse. The blessing if you obey the commandments of the Lord your God which I command you today and the curse, if you do not obey the commandments...' (Deuteronomy 11: 26–28)*

Justin clearly remembered the sermon and this day, even feared the consequences that were so very clearly explained by the preacher. Nevertheless, Justin with Sushmita had gone beyond the care of those well-established truths; the conviction in the spirit, as again felt by Justin on 'that day' was nowhere evident in practice. Somewhere it says that there is a way that seems right unto man but the end thereof is the ways of death. On this day, Justin was not able to see beyond the first half of the verse. He had conditioned himself to think that what he was planning with Sushmita was executable, workable and, ultimately, would be acceptable. They had started the final run to their pursuit of togetherness, which they thought was attainable.

They started making plans as to how both of them could get together and, at the same time, take care of Justin's responsibility towards the boys. They never discounted to give complete support to Pearl in her life afterwards. How these things would happen was anybody's guess. This would also mean that Justin would have to give up his ministerial work with the church so he started enhancing his skills in other vocations.

Without raising eyebrows, Justin very gradually started giving up his direct input in the church ministry and instead, started mentoring the able ministers from within the church to take up the lead role. For long, Justin had stopped the laying of hands on the church members for any reason. Instead, he would ask one of the co-pastors or the elders of the church to lay hands on members whenever the occasion arose. He firmly believed that by laying of hands, the anointing gets imparted to the other person. He was wary, lest anyone may receive the negative portion of his characteristic. He restricted his preaching the Word of God to a single Sunday in the month; instead, he would go out of his way to help the co-pastors to prepare their sermons for various church services.

Justin and Sushmita weighed their options and came to conclude that Justin should go and try to settle in America, while Sushmita should go back to her hometown in Bangalore. To look for job opportunities in America, Justin was banking upon his knowledge in the financial sector and his recently acquired computer skills. Sushmita, as a computer programmer, would not find it difficult to come across a suitable opening in her hometown. They both came to realise that they would have to wait for an opportune time and place to settle down together, and as such, they quietly started correspondence with their contacts with a view to further their plans.

Showdown

BY NOW, PEARL'S show of displeasure, though still subtle, was ever-present. The boys, at their tender age, did not know how to respond to such conspicuous developments. In fact, all the three in Justin's family always had very good and close relations with Sushmita, who was a frequent visitor to their house. There used to be frequent family visits from both sides on all occasions though, for the last few months, Justin started to feel the piercing eyes of Sushmita's aunt, Mrs. Goodwin, on his movements. In fact, in recent days, Mrs. Goodwin had clearly spoken her mind to Sushmita on the matter and there were scenes of strong disagreement between the two.

The resultant interaction between the two families dwindled and got limited to the church services. Justin and Sushmita very much regretted this, but nothing would deter them from the path they had set their hearts to follow.

Knock on the Door

THAT PARTICULAR DAY in June promised to be a scorcher. It was still morning and already Justin could see refraction in heat waves rising from the distant buildings which were bearing the brunt of the June sun beating down on them. The only place in Justin's house where one could let go a sigh of relief was right in front of the air-cooler, which ran with its big exhaust fan making a continuous humming rumble. Justin put his chair directly in the path of the cool breeze that the heavy-duty exhaust fan of the air-cooler was sucking from the *Khus* curtains (cooling straw), which were soaked by continuous stream of water. Justin could afford neither an air-conditioner nor the huge electricity bill that it would generate; so the air-cooler was his luxury.

With both the boys away at school and Pearl at work, Justin

had settled down with his Bible to read and meditate, when suddenly, the doorbell rang. Justin got up with great reluctance, for occasionally, street vendors would venture up the staircase of these apartment buildings and knock or ring the doorbell to promote their wares.

Justin opened the door and was about to reprimand the presumed street vendor for disturbing him, when he came face to face with very unusual visitors at this time of the morning: his four co-pastors from the church. Did the colour drain from his face? Yes, for sure, and he had a foreboding of a brewing storm. There was no reason for them to be here; *weren't they supposed to be at work right now...?* was the first thought that came to Justin's mind.

'Praise the Lord, brothers, what a surprise!' Justin said trying to keep his composure.

'Praise the Lord, brother', all replied in unison.

'Please make yourself comfortable while I serve you cold water. It is very hot today'" said Justin trying to calm down ominous thoughts crisscrossing his mind.

'No, brother, we are fine. Just come and sit with us for we wanted to talk to you on a particular matter', said the youngest of the four.

Justin had a very good idea of what was coming as he settled himself on his chair facing the four. For a few moments, the only comforting thing was the cool air coming out of the air-cooler, with its humming sound occasionally interrupted by the piercing chants of the vendors who were going about their business as usual on the street below.

Justin could see glances being exchanged between the four, coupled with hesitant expressions on their faces, probably deciding with unspoken words as to who should initiate the conversation.

After fidgeting in his seat several times, one of the co-pastors gathered the courage to say, 'Brother, we wanted to talk to you about Sushmita and yourself'.

Justin's mind froze for a few moments. It is amazing how a person can mentally traverse a whole lifetime of his past in a few seconds. As if detaching himself from the 'present', where his co-workers sought his attention, Justin scanned back all those years since he and Sushmita developed inordinate affection for each other, to until this day, when his co-pastors had ultimately gathered courage to broach upon this subject. Talking to himself, he thought, did he ever expect another ending to his 'adventure' or more appropriately 'misadventure'? However, for now, he had to shake himself out of this behavior of soliloquy, an act that he never committed to his own embarrassment or confusion of a passer-by.

'Oh!' was the only response he could muster.

Until now, Justin had always seen a very bright countenance on the faces of these ministers of his church. They were always full of energy, ever encouraging, trying to bear each other's burden whenever an occasion demanded. However, today, they looked dejected; though on a deeper probe into their eyes, Justin could also gauge an expectant spirit. That glimmer of expectancy in their eyes told Justin that they had not completely lost faith in him and were hopeful that this time of temptation could be overcome by prayerful discussion, and some of his exploits that were out of line could be wind down.

'Brother, we love you. All these years you have been our guide in the ministry, and we are sure things can once again be put in the right perspective', said one of the four, bending forward, resting his elbows on both his knees and holding his Bible in the hands.

The third interjected saying, 'The congregation loves you very much. Many of them have been spiritually born of you, and they all look towards you as their spiritual father. Till now, not many are in the know of all these things, but soon they will be able to read between the lines'.

'For the sake of God's work, the love of the congregation, your family and also for the good of Sushmita, we sincerely request that the two of you should choose separate ways', he continued to say, while looking towards others as if seeking their approval.

Giving a pause, possibly thinking things through his mind, he concluded his speech projecting assurance and comfort to Justin and said, 'You don't have to worry about Sushmita for we would talk to her privately. If you are ready to retrace your steps, we are sure she would be left with no option but to go along with your decision. Moreover, she is young and has her whole life ahead of her. In due course, she would find a good match for herself and settle down in life'.

Expressionless, Justin sat twiddling his thumbs and then, crossing his hands behind his head, he very gently started rocking his revolving chair back and forth.

Church Ministers

AS IF GOING through a time machine while the eyes of the four co-pastors beheld him expectantly, Justin transported himself to those moments when at different ministerial times, each one of them was encouraged by him to take a step of faith and dedicate their lives for a more active role in the church ministry.

Justin could vividly remember the time when, in one of the home fellowships, he had laid his hands on Arvind, a tall, middle-aged, soft spoken and prayerful man, and prompted him to prepare himself to be a part of the church ministry. Arvind accepted the word of wisdom, started praying in real earnest, and very soon, dedicated himself to become one of the co-pastors of the church. Arvind was always well-respected and loved by the congregants.

The second co-pastor, Ashok, was a stoutly built man with an ever-present soft and benevolent expression on his face. His demeanour defied the vocation that he pursued, which was operating heavy machinery. He had the listener's ear and whenever he needed to put forth his point of view, it was always with great clarity and straightforwardness. With the bible tucked securely under his arm, he was always there ready to help, ready to pray. Compared to the other main ministers of the church, Ashok sought God steadfastly through prayer and fasting. He was, 'the man on his knees'. People would flock around him after the church meetings requesting for intercessory prayers on their behalf.

Cyril, the third co-pastor, was a frail-looking man who, at times, seemed to easily get molded by the opinions of others; but strangely enough, capable of bringing forth his individual view when none was expected. After Justin, if an occasion demanded that someone may lead the way, the other co-pastors looked upon this feeble-structured man to take the initiative, and he never disappointed in that role.

Ravi, the fourth co-pastor, was the youngest of the lot. He was highly educated in his secular vocations with various degrees and diplomas tucked under his belt. His presentations were forceful, an art that he had learnt in the boardrooms of corporate offices. Usually dressed in his casuals and jeans, instead of the dress code as promoted by Justin and the other three, this young man manifested his anointing on various occasions while preaching in the church or other church-cell meetings. Ravi's unassuming character was popular with the younger crowd of the church, yet he was a person whose personality commanded recognition amongst the elders as well.

Justin's train of thoughts was disturbed by Arvind whose voice seemed to echo from a distance, 'Brother, we would like to hear from you in the matter. Our approach may have antagonised you, but we have come as your well-wishers and co-laborers in this ministerial work'.

This was one of those few occasions in Justin's life from which he could neither wiggle out nor wish it away. Many years back when he was young and was taking a shower in the bathroom, he observed a strange occurrence that scared him a lot and left indelible mark upon him. On one side of the bathroom, there was a window covered with wire-mesh that opened towards a shaft, which ran vertical to the building. The shaft was used as an air vent for the bathrooms of all the flats situated on this four-storied building. The shaft also had plumbing pipes running from top to bottom. These pipes, with the connecting bends and the T's, were a convenient resting place for pigeons and some other small birds. The shaft was open at the top and, during the day, was well lit by natural light. In the shower, Justin always enjoyed the crooning of the pigeons and the small tap dance that they would do by swaying from one side to another. Some time, they would move in a circular motion on their feet at the same spot, once clockwise, then anti-clockwise, and then again the tap dance.

On this particular day, while taking a shower, Justin was observing the dance of this particular pigeon sitting on the windowsill, when all of a sudden, he saw that the crooning and the dancing of the pigeon stopped abruptly and it shut its eyes. The eyes were shut so tight that Justin could clearly observe the whitish eyelids of the pigeon against its grey-feathered skin. Midway Justin stopped his activity of playing with the soapy lather and with eyes partly covered with the soap lather, he strained to see what was happening. All of a sudden—to the horror of Justin—in that flicker of a moment, a cat pounced on the pigeon and caught it by its neck. The feathers of the bird flew everywhere in the shaft and in the very next moment, the cat with its prey in its mouth was gone. Till date, Justin remembers his shriek and the fright he experienced for many days.

Today, the same emotions surged through him and he wished

the situation to disappear at the closing of his eyes. To his discomfort, they did not vanish, but to his relief, his co-pastors were not like cats pouncing upon him, but those who came to him with noble intentions and the spirit of humility.

'What do you expect me to say?' asked Justin.

'Brother, you are wise enough. We just wish that you should make the right decision and take up the path of restoration', said Ashok. 'We are with you to support you with our prayers'.

Justin knew that, today, he would have to spell out the course of his life. From the day Sushmita's mother, during her visit to the city of Delhi, repeatedly reprimanded her on the relationship with her pastor, Justin and Sushmita started thinking things through. They started discussing various scenarios that could confront them, whether in the church or through family members. In fact, every time their confrontation with members of either of their families became more unpleasant, their commitment to each other became stronger. They had come to the stage where they could no longer disown each other, whatever the cost may be.

They had started to probe life outside the church circle; where and how it would be, they both did not know. On several occasions, the two had discussed the probable process of divorce between Pearl and Justin and how they would have to go about it in a discreet manner—whatever that meant. Divorce and discreet! How that was possible was anybody's guess. Neither had an answer to such questions. The one thing that they had decided upon in all these uncertainties was to stick together through the thick and thin.

That day was the first time Justin had come face-to-face with this situation. His co-pastors, unaware of all that had transpired between Justin and Sushmita, were waiting to hear something encouraging from Justin, their Senior Pastor. The Bible was full of examples of famous biblical characters who erred but then repented and started afresh, but Justin was choosing a different path.

'Yes, they made their hearts like flint, refusing to hear the law and the words which the Lord of hosts had sent by His Spirit through the former prophets...'. (Zechariah 7: 12)

It is never easy to disappoint people who trust and depend upon you, and that day, Justin was standing in that very situation. With a heavy heart, he was preparing himself to make them come face-to-face with the harsh reality that he was about to tell. He loved all these people whom he had encouraged in the past to come forward in the church ministry. He had groomed them and laid his hands on them while inducting them in the ministerial work. For all these years, they had prayed for each other, carried each other's burden; they had been together through many ups and downs in this ministerial journey. In the church, they had built new relations that at times, proved to be stronger than natural relations were. He was about to jolt them out of the interdependence they had built through faith upon God and upon each other. As the saying goes, life is not always a bed of roses. In spite his best intentions, today, Justin was at a point in life, where he was about to agonise everyone.

He made his heart like flint, devoid of any emotions, and said, 'Brothers, I love you all, and I am very sure that you do believe this. I am sure you also trust that I have been truly trying to serve God. However, with a very heavy heart, I want to confess that what you have said is true; Sushmita and I have developed affection for each other and we will not be able to change this equation'.

Concerns

'WHAT WILL HAPPEN to your family, brother?' they asked in unison.

'Well, I and my family have not discussed this as yet, but soon we will come to some conclusion', was Justin's reply.

'What will happen to the church?'

'Brothers, the church is not dependent upon one person; it is the Body of Christ and He has raised able ministers who would carry the work forward. I have faltered and I must leave. You would have noticed that for quite some time, I had relinquished the charge of the church and you people have been managing the affairs. That is how a church or any other organisation should work—whoever is not able to carry on the responsibilities in spite of one's commitment must go. The church is not standing on one pillar, there are many pillars that support this structure and the responsibilities should be taken over by them', Justin explained further.

'Brother, is it that easy to replace a leader? Is it that easy to just go and tell the congregation that Pastor Justin will not be with us anymore? You must take all these things into account before making a final decision', pleaded one of them.

The youngest one said, 'What will the outside world say, what will we tell them? Do we tell them that our senior pastor has given up God's work in pursuit of his worldly desires?'

'What will become of this church? Who would like to come to attend our services after this? You are not giving a thought to anyone else, except yourself. Brother, you must think it over again', he continued in an agitated voice.

The heat was picking up for Justin. He did not have an answer to any of those questions. There was no way to justify his own missteps. He was their culprit and he knew he was leaving them in a lurch. They were probably better off in their own vocations as nominal Christians before they had met Justin. Many years ago, Justin was the one who, discerning the anointing upon these men had encouraged each at different times to take up the higher calling. With grace, all in the past had received the vision that Justin imparted to them about the church ministry. They had started taking out time after their secular vocations to devote themselves to the ministerial work in the church. At times, they would cut into their family time but would keep pressing on, never looking back even once and today; their mentor himself wanted to leave them midway. This was criminal, it was deceit, and it was leaving people orphaned.

In spite of the fear of facing ridicule, stiff opposition from families and friends, and being displaced from their respective vocations, Sushmita and Justin had been quietly preparing themselves for such an eventuality. They knew that they were going to break many-a-heart and the church system, as an institution, would suffer because of their selfish and so to say aberrant actions. Basic trust of people in whom they believe would become debatable, but with no ambiguity in their minds, Justin and Sushmita had prepared themselves to go ahead and eventually fulfill their desire of living together. For the purpose of their togetherness, they had decided to jeopardise the togetherness of families, friends and community as a whole.

The Bible says, 'A man who isolates himself seeks his own desire; He rages against all wise judgment'. (Proverbs 18: 1)

To deter any further counsels, requests, pleadings or hidden admonish, Justin said with finality in his voice, 'Brothers, I respect each one of you and value everything that you have said, but let me once again repeat that I cannot give up my relations with Sushmita. I will also not be available from now onwards to take the responsibility of any lead role in the church'.

They were crest-fallen. There was complete silence in the room that seemed to drag for an eternity when, ultimately, the youngest co-pastor Ravi said, 'Brother, you don't have any fear of the Lord'.

Resignation writ large on their faces, heads hanging and shoulders drooping, they left. Justin had a heavy heart but somewhere he felt as if he has achieved something that he coveted. It being, the first step towards togetherness with Sushmita.

HOW CAN THEY?

BIDING THEIR TIME, Sushmita and Justin waited to see the response the meeting would have once the co-pastors decided to brief the people who mattered the most. However, after a couple of days when they did not encounter any unwanted attention from anyone in the families or from the church members, they made out that his co-pastors had not divulged the details yet to anyone.

Then one day, out of blue, Justin received a telephone call from Ravi, the youngest co-pastor, who wanted him to come to his house along with Sushmita. There he proposed to call another elderly pastor, fondly known as *Sadhu*[12] *ji*, who had been a guest preacher in some of their church meetings. Justin was skeptical at first, but then decided to go there with Sushmita. To him, this seemed like a step forward where someone was calling them together and in the process acknowledging their relationship.

On the way, Justin and Sushmita were rather subdued for they did not know the real purpose behind the meeting. Throughout the drive, Sushmita sat close to Justin resting her head on his shoulders, the only thing they confirmed again in not so many words was their commitment towards each other. Having come

---

12 A person who has relinquished social comforts/status to follow the path of a religion

so far, they did not want anyone to raise false hope of their going separate ways. Their resolve was firm.

Not affiliated to any church or denomination, this elderly man, the *Sadhu ji*, preached the Bible with the freedom of spirit, wherever he was invited. He always wore a white *khadi kurta* and *dhoti* with an open *sandal* modelled after the Gandhian dress code. Sporting a dense, white moustache that merged with the long, flowing white beard, he commanded respect and attention for the aura he thus created around him. He was well-versed with the Bible. Extensively travelled, this elderly preacher was bold and straightforward. Driving towards the residence of Ravi, Justin and Sushmita remembered an instance when *Sadhu ji* was preaching in one of their church meetings and faltered in his speech.

Justin was always articulate with his speech. He was careful about the way he spoke and even in his carefree moments, his speech did not falter. He attributed this quality to his mother and to his father, respectively, but for entirely different reasons. To his mother, for she was the most soft-spoken person, he had ever known. Except for the times when he was very young and would indulge in some silly activity, she would raise her voice, accompanied with the raised index finger of her right hand, which used to serve as the warning for what would otherwise follow as the result of continuous defiance.

For corporal punishments, as and when demanded according to the act committed, she had reserved a red, two-foot long foot-ruler that was kept safely in one corner of their house. Justin and his younger sister, though very close to each other in age, would always wait for such opportunity when their mother would need that correction rod for either of them. At such times, sibling rivalry came to the fore and the other would run to fetch the fearsome red stick and respectfully put it in the hands of their mother, before pulling back to a safe distance. Their mother would then wave the scale in the air quite a few times giving the most fearsome impression; however, the strike with it would not be more than a tap on the palm of their hands and that was the extent their mother would go to punish them.

Their father, on the other hand, had seen action on the Burma front in the late forties. Stoutly built, he had a commanding voice that of an Indian army *subedar* (in-charge of five to ten soldiers). Justin did not remember ever being hit by his father, but would tremble at his thundering voice that sounded as if he was giving marching orders to his soldiers. Justin always feared and resented his voice, which in its most subtle form was also like a war cry.

At that very young age itself, Justin had decided that he would never raise his voice and be aggressive, but would follow the way his mother conducted herself.

He remembered to have broken this pattern only once in his life when, during college, he was attending an NCC (National Cadet Corp) camp conducted in the desert city of *Sardar Shahar* in Rajasthan. He was an under-officer cadet in the NCC and realised that, while commanding a big squad of more than 200 cadets, his soft-spoken attitude did not work to his advantage. It was at that time, the 'once in lifetime' occasion, that he screamed orders to his squad at the top of his voice. Not only did he resort to shouting at the top of his voice, but also learnt quite a few curse words that he used frequently in that NCC camp to command respect from the fellow cadets. That was his only brush with a loud voice accompanied with cursing. The soft-spoken attitude that he had nurtured all those years always put him in advantage and even in his carefree moments; he did not falter.

On the other hand, this *Sadhu ji* with his white flowing beard, while preaching in one of the church meetings, inadvertently used a mild curse word that left everyone aghast with disbelief.

On that day while going to meet Ravi his co-pastor, Justin had purposely asked Sushmita to wear a sari, so that she may look more mature. At the sound of the approaching car, Ravi came out to receive Justin and Sushmita and after the exchange of pleasantries, they all proceeded to the living room of his apartment. After they settled down, Ravi sent all his family members to the other room, leaving Justin and Sushmita with himself and *Sadhu ji*.

Ravi briefed *Sadhu Ji* of all that the co-pastors had talked to Justin in their last meeting and that it was the first time anyone was approaching Sushmita in the matter. To Justin's surprise, Sushmita was sitting very confidently and intently listening to the conversation.

After the introductory talk, all of a sudden, Ravi directed a question at Sushmita, 'Sister, how long do you know our Pastor?'

'As long as you know him', was her curt reply.

'No, I mean how long you know him otherwise, I mean in a different way. You know what I mean', said Ravi in an uncomfortable way.

'Yes I know what you mean, and now I know him "well" for quite a few years', was Sushmita's unhesitant reply.

'Pastor, what you have to say?' Ravi said turning towards Justin.

'You already know my position, Ravi.'

'Knowing all the complications that you two would have to undergo, regarding the divorce of the Pastor couple, antagonising so many people in the church, don't you two think that giving up each other is a smaller sacrifice that this demands?" said *Sadhu Ji* while caressing his long beard in a very thoughtful way.

'*Sadhu Ji*, we have come too far to retrace our steps. I know what we are doing is not in the interest of anyone and may be not in our own interest either, but we are past that stage from where we can turn back', said Justin trying to explain their point of view.

'What stage you are talking about that you have crossed?' asked *Sadhu Ji*.

'He means we are so close to each other now that we cannot turn back', Sushmita interjected trying to come to Justin's rescue.

'I feel that you can always turn back provided you have not reached a certain point in this relationship', said *Sadhu Ji*.

'What I mean is that people of opposite sex do so many

things together which they should not be doing but everything can be ignored, forgiven, put behind provided they have not reached that stage in their relationship which will be really termed as adultery', he continued.

In spite of all his shortcomings, until now, Justin has held onto the unspoken teaching of his mother and, and he and Sushmita though being very close to each other for the last so many years have never even contemplated crossing all limits in their relationship. Justin knew exactly what the Bible says about adultery and he felt that *Sadhu Ji* was diluting the severity of sin of sexual lust—provided the final act was not committed.

However, Justin could make out in his mind that if he said that they had not committed that final act, then these people would further pressurise them emotionally, to part company. So Justin said on behalf of Sushmita and himself, 'Yes, we are past that'.

'Oh, then nothing can be done', was a precise but curt reply of *Sadhu Ji*.

Justin was aghast by the strange way they were approaching this matter. How can they put sin in various categories? Though, they were trying to find a way out for the benefit of Justin and Sushmita, he knew that lust of the flesh does not have to be brought to the point of consummation to be called adultery. The Bible clearly tells that even looking at the opposite sex and lusting-after in the heart is adultery? You are a sinner and want to remain one, fine! So be it but what is written in the Bible cannot be diluted. Justin was now arguing against himself.

Anything outside marriage is sin. Anyone who gets into a relationship with another married person is committing a sin. What is this talk of levels? To what extent one goes in the relationship outside marriage does not make one more or less of a sinner. Sin is sin until it is acknowledged and repented, simple as that.

That was the end of their meeting with Ravi and *Sadhu ji*.

AU REVOIR

THE DAY HAD come for Justin to board the plane from Indira Gandhi International Airport for a flight to America where his sister, who had sponsored him, lived. Many people from the church had come to see him off, for they understood that Justin, their pastor, was just going to visit his sister and was to come back in a few months. This was part of the arrangement made between Justin and the select church leaders. As it would give them sufficient time to gradually take over the responsibilities of the church, and on the other hand, Justin's departure would not look like as if he was abandoning the church.

Pearl, in her childhood, had always trusted the man who was her father. There was never an occasion in her life when she could not put her trust in him. She always felt carefree while under his roof. After marriage, Pearl had put her entire trust in Justin, her husband. The first twenty years of their married life were blissful. Justin had completely replaced her father in all aspects of trust, confidence, dependability, gentleness and always proved to be a very good husband. She was very happy and content until the time Justin was working for the bank. Soon after Justin had resigned from his bank's job to take up full-time ministry with the church, their family came in close contact with Sushmita and lo and behold, much time did not pass when Pearl noticed questionable closeness developing between Sushmita and Justin. Right from the beginning, she tried hard to make Justin understand at each step that what he was doing was not right. In fact, she even went to the extent of clearly telling him that his inordinate affection towards Sushmita was sinful. She never blamed Sushmita for anything, for in her eyes, Justin, being a pastor and the more mature person was responsible for everything. She repeatedly told him that he had become covetous about Sushmita, junior to him by many years.

The scripture says,

> 'He who is greedy for gain troubles his own house...'.
> (Proverbs 15: 27)

Apart from Justin, Pearl used to blame Satan in her heart for alluring Justin towards Sushmita so that the Lord's work may be hampered. She had known Justin for the last twenty years and until then, she always found him to be a faithful and responsible man and a very good father to their two boys.

Pearl had traveled a long way in her life—from being content, to now being disheartened and distraught. From being the wife of a trustworthy man, to now living with the same man who had closed his eyes to all good counsel. She had gone from the phase of a woman who held her head high in the society, to the one who felt pity for herself. From being a very warm and lively person, to the one whose heart always hurt. She underwent all the turmoil, but never complaint to anyone about Justin. This was her family, this was her life, and this was her man, to whom she could complain? These were the times when she missed her father. Oh! How she desired that he be around, she could have confided in him. Even though she knew, he also could not have done much, except pray.

Throughout her twenty years of married life, Justin sheltered her. She had never travelled by herself except to her office. She had practically never gone out of the house without Justin; he was overprotective about her and she adored the feeling. Without him, it seemed she did not know anything about the world. After

God, this was the man she trusted the most. As a pastor couple, often, they used to go to counsel and strengthen other people who were going through a difficult patch in their lives, and today she herself felt tortured by those very circumstances out of which she uplifted others. Pearl then started to realise that it was getting all the more difficult for Justin and her to get back into the loving relationship that was once the reason of her joy and happiness.

Justin had even mentioned divorce to which she had replied with disgust, 'Go ahead and do whatever you like'. Her mind had stopped working. She was on the brink of losing her inner sanctity though, outwardly, she kept her demeanor for the sake of her boys.

That day, standing at the airport, to bid Justin adieu, she was hoping within herself that the distance of continents which would now physically separate Sushmita and Justin might gradually dampen their passion for each other.

At the airport Armaan, the younger son, stuck to Justin's side continuously, not leaving his father even for a moment. Shades of emotions alternating between excitement and apprehension appeared on his face. At the age of twelve, he was excited to be at the airport but apprehensive at the same time, for his father, whom he loved dearly, would be gone for quite a few months. Armaan has never been without his father, even for a day. Standing next to him, the young boy was shaking with emotions upon which he had no control. Repeatedly, Justin put his arms around him trying to comfort him but in turn he kept asking one question, 'Papa, when will you come back?'

'Do not worry, son! I will be back very soon, and when I come back, I will bring for you lots of things that you like'.

Ultimately, the time to board the plane had come and Justin had to part company with Armaan, Rahul, and Pearl. He saw them huddle together; however, in spite of their closeness, he could feel Armaan standing on his own with shadows of deep sadness in his eyes, not even wanting to take the comforting support of his mother or elder brother. A stab of pain rose sharply in Justin's heart.

TRANSITION

THE PLANE MOVED into the European air space and then, after a short stopover at Vienna, the journey towards the land of opportunities called 'America' continued.

It was daytime when the plane entered the air space over the Atlantic sea, the water-body separating America from Europe. The seat belt sign was turned off and the service people started moving down the aisle of the aircraft, stopping at each row and curtly enquiring of the occupants as to their preference of drinks. Justin asked for a chilled can of soda along with a peanut sachet. He was amused at the airline's offer of peanuts, which is considered the cheapest among dry fruits in India. He nestled his soda can in the receptacle of the arm of his seat, occasionally sipping from it in between carefully picking up a peanut and tossing it into his mouth. Flying through the cirrus formation of clouds was like floating through a dreamland, and for a few hours, Justin was lost in his thoughts.

The announcement on the intercom jolted him out of his dreams, and he heard that the plane was about fifteen minutes away from New York airport. Justin straightened up in his seat and excitedly looked out of the window and there, far ahead, he saw the shoreline of the land called 'America'. Soon, Justin could also see the big skyscrapers that made up the skyline of New York

City. He could feel in his spirit that this was going to be a new beginning of his life. Once out of the immigration area, he proceeded to catch a connecting flight to Oklahoma City to be with his sister, Urmila.

Once the initial euphoria of being in America was over, Justin found that even after four months he had not come across any employment opportunity that would give him hope and as such was completely dependent on his sister.

His sister, Urmila, was a very religious, hardworking and a God-fearing individual. She had migrated to America in the late seventies. After going through a rough patch in her married life, she now lived as a single mother of two young children, still trying to achieve the 'American Dream'. Although, she *did* own an average-sized ranch style house with many amenities that were still a dream for a similarly placed family in India, but to cope up with the monthly bills and payments for all those household gadgets of envy, she would many a times work at a second job or stay late for an extra shift. Very soon, Justin learned that living paycheck-to-paycheck was the norm for most people in this country and all those extra dollars were needed to be earned to pay the creditors, car loans, house mortgages, etc. The working conditions were far more stringent here compared to India.

Oftentimes, Urmila, would get flustered when it would take a lot of effort on part of her two children to get used to calling Justin as 'Uncle' instead of calling him by his first name, as was the norm there. For Justin, his own name sounded so alien because back in India no one called him by his first name. He was Brother Justin for church people and Mr. Justin for others; the younger generation there would simply call him 'Uncle'.

On Sunday mornings, Urmila used to go to a nearby town where she attended a charismatic evangelical church. The congregants of that church accounted for one-third of the population of the small town. Justin noted that most of the congregants of the church were predominantly white and his sister's family was the only one of an Asian origin. Some of the church members worked in big offices in nearby cities, a few drove eighteen-wheeler trailer trucks, some were teachers, others worked in the nearby malls, some worked as butchers in meat shops and a couple of them were in the sanitation department. This seemed to be a completely integrated society—under one roof, devoid of any class stigma. This was quite unlike India where, even in this millennium, one could not find such a unified social gathering.

There was class system still prevalent everywhere in India. Like the railways, where there were different categories for travel in the train that was created according to one's affluence; or even take a movie theater, where people were segregated according to the amount of money they could pay at the ticket booth.

A butcher in India would never like his child to be identified in the school by the vocation of the father. A truck driver's role in the society was defined by his vocation and not what he was as a person, and the people working in the sanitation department were a different class by itself. Even today, the world being completely engulfed in the changes being envisioned by the after effects of the Arab-spring, this category of people in India had to be content with the prefix of 'schedule-caste' to their names, defining their status across the length and breadth of the country. Indian politicians would not let go this casteism at any cost. Even in this era of Martian landing, they needed the cast factor to evoke passions during the elections, the by-elections, the loksabha elections, the municipal elections, the assembly elections, the *panchayat* elections[13], the *gram panchayat* elections, the *zila parishad* elections and the likes; you name it and you have got one. In spite of the enormous progress made by India in almost every sphere, the caste-system bedeviled the roots of world's greatest democracy.

Justin noted that in America, class-difference, dependent

---

13 District/Block governing bodies

on social strata was not much pronounced, and may even be termed as non-existent amongst the general populace; however, on scrutiny, one could find some undercurrents based on differences in nationalities and colour. Justin's observation in this regard was based on his limited exposure to the American society. He gradually started noticing that though the church people seemed to mingle during the service, their interaction on a social level after the service narrowed down to nationality, ethnicity and even colour. This was evident as his sister who was a member of this church for the last twenty years, had minimal social interaction with the church members. He observed that after the initial exchange of pleasantries with the church members over coffee after the service, or the customary exchange of notes on the weather, he and his sister would practically be standing by themselves. Topics of common interest between his sister and the other congregants were literally non-existent. Justin did not think that the pastor fell in the same category, for he always went out of his way to make them feel comfortable.

After all, even Americans were not completely untouched by this globally inherent nature of human beings—segregating themselves on the basis of race, colour, nationalities, etc. In fact, segregating oneself is not as bad as harboring a biased opinion against each other is. Here in America, even though the demarcation of race, colour and nationalities seemed somewhat blurred and such practices vehemently opposed, one could definitely feel the undercurrents.

The very first thing that God thought and said while creating human race is amply clear from the scriptures:

Then God said, 'Let Us make man in our image, according to our likeness…'. (Genesis 1: 26)

It seems that nowhere in the world, be it developed world, developing world or the third world countries, the concept that everyone is created by God after His own image and likeness is really and truly understood and appreciated by us humans, to shun any thought of preeminence over each other. Even the nomenclature 'developed world, developing world and the third world countries' smacks of a great divide in the mind set of human beings.

Justin felt slightly uncomfortable at times by the show of this attitude in this great country. To him, America was the embodiment of Christianity, modernism, tolerance, generosity, fraternity, liberty, equality and all good things about life he learnt over the years. However, in this short span of four months, Justin got very disillusioned about Christianity and equality in America. Even though there were a lot of church buildings, he did not see Christian values being lived here. 'Equality', with respect to races and nationalities, of which America is the main proponent, seemed to have very weak bearing in the society at large.

ACROSS THE CONTINENTS

COMMUNICATING ACROSS THE continents using a landline was a costly preposition, so Justin's sister bought him a few calling cards, which enabled him to make frequent phone calls to India. However, finding alone time to call Sushmita without his sister's knowledge was a difficult task. Whenever he wanted to make a call to India, his sister would presume, that he was calling Pearl and the boys, and always wanted to say hello to them. In order to talk to Sushmita, without any disturbance, Justin would have to wait until late night, when everyone would go to sleep.

Whenever Justin could talk to Sushmita over the phone, it was like young lovers torn apart by the distance. For many days, they just whispered sweet nothings in each other's ears that made them happy, but then Justin realised that Sushmita was becoming more assertive and started questioning him about progress at his end and how long would she would have to wait before they could get married. Being a young woman in her late twenties, Sushmita wanted to talk freely about Justin with her friends in Bangalore but that was not possible as they were still not clear about the shape of things to come. Moreover, Sushmita was in her hometown and the pressure from her family to get married was immense. Her family was constantly bombarding her with new marriage alliances that constantly put her in an awkward position as she was forced to reject them all, in turn raising many eyebrows.

AN OPENING

NEARLY FOUR MONTHS had gone by since Justin came to America and nothing much was in sight in terms of job opportunities, but Justin prayerfully kept waiting for things to happen.

All this while, Justin's exposure in the church at Oklahoma increased and on a few occasions during the church service, the Pastor asked him to share 'The Word' from the Bible. These times were very precious for Justin, as his passion to preach the Word of God was finding an outlet. Very soon, the Pastor felt the anointing that rested on Justin to preach from the Bible. One Sunday morning after the church service, the Pastor called him in his office to discuss an important issue.

When Justin entered the church office, he found that all the elders of the church had also assembled there. Since the time Justin developed an affinity towards Sushmita, anything out of the ordinary sent shivers down his spine. Closed in this room with the Pastor and elders of the church, Justin felt as if it was a scene from the movie 'Hatari'. The Pastor, with his large frame, looked like John Wayne seated on the bonnet chair of a weather-beaten truck of the sixties wildly swinging a noose in his hands in hot pursuit of the rhinoceros that was cornered by other players in the game.

The Bible says, '...the sound of a shaken leaf shall cause

*them to flee; they shall flee as though fleeing from a sword,
and they shall fall when no one pursues.' (Leviticus 26: 36)*

Justin felt trapped whilst his mind started imagining every possible scenario as he slowly seated himself on the edge of a chair facing the Pastor.

'Justin, we have been talking about you for quite some time and have been pondering as to how we should deal with this matter', said the Pastor gesturing towards the elders.

It was unusually cold for the month of October, and the night before, it had snowed. In the morning, Justin could see icicles hanging outside at every conceivable place: the trees, the power lines, the mailbox. In fact, at home when he opened the outside door, transparent crystal like icicles broke off from the top of the door and fell on the floor in front of him. On this chilly winter afternoon, sitting in the church office, surrounded by a host of church elders, Justin felt sweat trickling down his back. He feared that the pallor of his face had probably given him away and he could barely muster the strength to say, 'What about it?'

'Justin, we would like to utilise your anointing in church ministry', said the Pastor, looking deep into Justin's eyes with an element of expectancy.

Justin who was holding his breath in the intervening period let out a sigh of relief. He was hoping that no one had noticed his uneasiness, then shifting uneasily from side to side, he settled deeper in the chair. Fear dissipated, Justin lifted his face and with a bemused expression, kept looking at the Pastor for him to elaborate upon his statement.

'Justin, the church always wanted to start a ministry in one of the cities with concentration of immigrants from Asian countries but the language barrier held us back. After you came, and at the manifestation of the anointing that is bestowed upon you to preach the Word from the Bible, we were contemplating if you would be interested in joining the church as a full-time minister and advance this ministry in the city of your choice'.

Without waiting for a response from Justin, the Pastor continued to say, 'Justin, we are serious about this work and if you decide to take up this ministry, we can sponsor you for an R1 visa, which would be good for a two-to-four-year period'.

Another elder of the church picked up the conversation saying, 'After you decide and we apply for the R1 visa, you may even become eligible for a green card in approximately four years'.

This was a pleasant surprise for Justin, but he knew that he needed to think it through. Preaching was his first passion and he was already feeling the void within himself for lack of opportunities to preach the Word of God.

After some pause, Justin said, 'Pastor, this is very encouraging, but I hope you would understand that I need some time to think it over'.

'Sure thing, Justin', the elders said in unison with the Pastor.

QUANDARY

I T WAS DUSK when Justin and Urmila started for home after that Sunday service. The wind was blowing very hard and the temperature dropped considerably. However, Justin was glad to come out of the church building, as the heat inside the centrally heated building was getting unbearable. The whiff of fresh air was invigorating. Justin was yet to learn how people in this country switched from their heavy winter gear while outdoors to just a shirt when indoors.

The snow on the roads within the city limits was shoveled but as they progressed to the narrow road that connected the town to the highway, driving became extremely tricky and dangerous.

On this snow-covered road, the traction control of the small, family sedan that his sister drove was unable to cope with the slippery conditions. Justin could literally see his sister's knuckles turn white because of the pressure she was applying to hold the steering.

The inclement weather conditions did not dampen the spirit of his sister who got very excited on hearing that the church was interested in utilising his services for ministerial work. Justin was her only brother and the only blood relative in this country apart from her two children. She had last visited India for the purpose of getting married. Within a couple of years, she got the news that their mother passed away, but was unable to attend the funeral, as her children were too young to be left in the care of others. She was thrilled by the news that the church was interested in inducting Justin in the ministry and would sponsor him for the purpose. She thought that if this offer materialised, then finally someone from her family circle would be with her in this country. All along the way, she excitedly talked about how nice it would be once Justin gets his green card and in a couple of years, his family can join him.

That night, Justin could not sleep. Weighing all pros and cons, he was eager to break this news to Sushmita. He was aware that the process for R1 visa could take a few months and after that, one has to wait for another three-four years to apply for a green card. This could be a good opening, but the process could be a long, drawn-out one. Sushmita, on the other hand, was already under pressure from her family to get married and she herself was getting impatient about it. She was of the opinion that either Justin should settle quickly in America so that she could join him there at the earliest, or he should simply come back to India and settle things there, once and for all.

NEW HORIZONS

WEIGHING ALL HIS options, Justin could clearly see that the offer made by the church was a God sent opportunity. This may really open doors for him to move forward with his passion to preach the Word of God and pave the way for him to settle down here in America. In due course, he would be eligible to apply for permanent resident status and subsequently be able to call Sushmita.

To the joy of his sister, Justin agreed to the proposal made by the church and opted to go to New York and begin church work there among the Asian Christians. His papers were filed and soon he received the religious visa without any obstacles.

Given the circumstances, Sushmita received the news of his R1 visa with both excitement and caution. She was happy because this would really mean that Justin would be able to call her to America and they could finally settle down in life. However, she was skeptical regarding the whole situation as it could prove to be a lengthy process.

In the face of it all, Sushmita put a condition in front of Justin that he should immediately seek divorce from his wife. This was the hardest part even though Justin knew all along that the path he was following would eventually necessitate this final step.

At Justin's departure from India, Pearl, although hoping against hope, was prepared to face the inevitable; so when, one day, she received a call from Justin on the subject of divorce, devoid of any emotions she agreed to go ahead with it. It was hard for everyone. The boys, particularly the younger one, were completely devastated by the state of affairs between their parents, but no one could stop the tide that was sweeping through their lives. Surprisingly, getting a divorce in New York was hassle-free and after receiving the affidavit from Pearl, it was smooth sailing. Pearl nearly stopped all kind of interaction with him, though Sushmita found this to be in her favour. She was quite pleased of the outcome and wanted to go ahead with plans for her life with Justin.

Justin, on the other hand, regularly kept in touch with his sons, taking care of all their needs in spite of the limited income from the church. Initially, Justin resided with one of the church families but then he arranged to live as a paying guest with one of the Gujarati families in the Jackson Heights area, in the borough of Queens.

There were quite a few people living in that three-story building owned by the Gujarati family. Since Justin needed to have some privacy for the purpose of meditating on Bible, the Landlord, affectionately known as 'Golu Bhai', very generously offered him a 9'x7'x7' unused laundry room to make his home. Justin was much pleased with the privacy that he could enjoy with the money that he was able to spare for his boarding and lodging. In spite of living in a spacious house all his life, Justin, surprisingly, found it very easy to adapt to this life style. The laundry room was near the back alley, and he always found an old neighbour trying to peek inside through the window. 'Golu Bhai' had cautioned Justin saying that the man was a troublemaker, who enjoyed reporting to the authorities about the living condi-tions of the tenants of this building. Justin always took extra care that no noise filtered out from his room and ensured that the curtains of the room were kept drawn to keep off the prying eyes. He did not want to lose this heavenly abode.

His church members were very generous and would always offer him a ride to the church on Sunday mornings. After the church service, he would invariably end up with one of the church families and after having evening meals with them would return to his retreat.

In spite of living in America, Justin's finances were very tight. He observed that to supplement their income, other Asian church pastors opted to work with various car services. Falling in line with his likes, Justin also started working for a car company to bolster his finances. This helped Justin with the finances to some extent even though the cost of running the car was exorbitant. Justin realised that back in India, Pearl's income would not be sufficient to take care of all her household expenses, so he made sure to send money on a regular basis for the upkeep of his sons. Sushmita, however, did not favour the idea for Justin's continued support to Pearl and the family after the divorce. She began pressurising Justin to call her to America at the earliest. Justin explored all possible avenues to get Sushmita a job in some software company in America so that she may get a work visa, but alas, it was not to be so. As far as Justin was concerned, there was no way for him to get a green card before certain immigration requirements were fulfilled, which would take a couple of years.

A Shocker His Way

THE CITY OF Manhattan was all spruced up for the holiday season and this was Justin's second winter in America. Sitting on a cheap plastic chair in his room, with the luxury of a small electric heater, he proceeded to call Sushmita as per the routine that they were following for the last one and a half years. To his surprise, after calling her cell number repeatedly, he did not get any response; it seemed the phone was switched off. This was rather unusual, as she always answered his phone call at the very first ring. That night, he could not get a wink of sleep and repeatedly called Sushmita but all in vain.

The next day was a repeat performance of the night before and again, Justin did not sleep. He was in no position to call anybody else and enquire about Sushmita's well-being. This kept on going for another ten days, by the end of which Justin was a sleep-deprived emotional wreck.

On the night of the eleventh day, Justin's call went through and the moment Sushmita came on line, he burst out asking all sorts of questions in one breath, 'Where have you been, what happened to you, is everything okay at your end?'

Justin was agonisingly surprised at the cool response he got from Sushmita when she said, 'Everything is okay, and I had just gone away on a vacation with one of my friends'.

This struck Justin as an extremely odd explanation and he realised that something was amiss.

'Why didn't you tell me? And who is this friend with whom you went on a vacation?'

'I went to a hill station with a guy friend',” was her terse reply.

Stunned for a few minutes, Justin could not say anything.

Then taking control of himself he asked, 'Sushmita, what's going on?'

Unfazed Sushmita replied dryly, 'I need my space'.

Justin felt as if she was talking in an alien language and he was unable to make any sense out of it, but he tried to keep his cool and asked, 'What is this "space" thing?'

'I just need my space and I do not think that I want to talk to you anymore', said Sushmita in a firm voice and after that with a beep of the phone, she hung up.

He tried calling her back immediately but she did not pick up the phone. Justin felt as if the whole earth was spinning around him. He could not believe his ears, he felt sick to the stomach. His hand let go off the cell phone and he slowly sank in his bed. Lying on his bed, he felt as if the ceiling was closing in on him.

With a startled expression on his face, he jumped out of the bed and sat on the plastic chair. He had never felt so helpless!

Years ago, when Justin was not even a teenager, standing amidst a crowd, sometimes he would have this weird feeling and would often ask himself if everything around him was real, or if he was alive, or if whatever was going on around him made any sense. Today, after so many years, encompassed by the same feeling, he asked himself whether he was alive or if everything around him was real. His brain felt numb. He lay down on the bed one more time and for hours together kept staring back at the low ceiling that seemed to spin from time to time. Finally, feeling too exhausted, he fell asleep.

The following day, he tried calling Sushmita several times but to his dismay, she did not care to pick up the phone. Justin was still not able to accept the fact that Sushmita had walked out on him. He was not even in a position to fly back to India to confront Sushmita. This is the tragedy of America—one cannot fly back to one's native place as and when needed, be it marriage, a birthday, an anniversary, even a death. In his case, though it was a matter of life and death, Justin was not in a position to leave the country as he was on an R1 visa and travelling at this time was not advisable. Taking the risk of going to India and not be able to travel back was not something Justin was ready to do. He doubted if he would even be able to meet or speak to Sushmita in her present state of mind. The thought of Sushmita vacationing with another guy on a hill station nauseated him repeatedly. How could she do that to him? In those moments of anguish, it dawned upon him how much Pearl must have suffered by his extramarital affair with Sushmita. He was being paid back in the same coin. The person whom he trusted more than life itself had betrayed him, someone for whom he had jeopardised his name, fame, family and much more; that very person in all likelihood had given up on him for another person. He chose Sushmita over hundreds of his church members who put their trust in him over the years. He chose

Sushmita over his boys; the bringing up of whom and their stability in life depended upon him. He chose Sushmita over Pearl, for whom he meant everything. The biggest betrayal being that he chose Sushmita over God himself, forsaking and denying him in front of the whole world. That person, Sushmita, had now cut all cords with him. Walking with Sushmita, Justin had walked away from everything that mattered in life, and now, Sushmita had walked out on him.

THE BUBBLE

WHILE JUSTIN WAS undergoing the traumatic experience of his life, the financial world was busy creating another tower of Babel at that time. The money managers had come together with singleness of mind, which was not witnessed in recent times and were busy blowing a financial bubble, by raising the stakes to unprecedented levels and in uncharted territory. These investment portfolio builders and hedge fund managers working with big financial institutions were like puppeteers sitting atop the bubble—throwing down lines to the people standing below, exhorting all and sundry to hold the line and climb to the top of the world. Well, many took the bait with dreams of making it big in the financial world and now there was an ecstatic multitude of hopefuls sitting atop the financial bubble. Literally, the whole world was drawn unto this bubble, which could not be contained by geographical boundaries of the nations of the world. Justin was no exception to the euphoria.

A bubble cannot withstand pressure, neither from the inside nor the outside. The money managers with their suaveness were raising the stakes which kept bloating the bubble to dangerous dimensions. The stock values were touching sky high and real estate was taking the property value to dizzy heights. At any given time, stretch limousines could be seen making rounds of Manhattan, the city that was the showpiece on the earth. The crazed occupants in those limousines were enjoying the sights of the famed Broadway and Times Square by popping their heads out of the moon-roof. They were busy clicking away at nothing and everything with their compact digital cameras, hollering at the same time to attract attention of the passerby to show that they could afford the luxury.

The streetwalkers—the lesser mortals—were amazed, walking wide-eyed as if in a stupor at the show of this affluence on their streets. Wine and food was in abundance in the hotels that were bursting at the seams with patrons at all hours of the day. Garbage trucks feverishly worked overtime during night shifts to remove the huge black garbage bags that piled up on the sidewalk due to great consumption and leftovers that were generated by the indulgence of the rich and the famous. Construction activity was at its crescendo and one could see huge construction cranes propped up everywhere, with quite a few malfunctioning every now and then, causing accidents and even deaths.

A 'bubble' is something which has virtual mass inside. No real mass, no real substance—'Nada'. One day, all of a sudden because of the great pressure that built up, the 'bubble' burst and the multitude of people sitting atop and enjoying the worldview fell to the ground with a great thud. The fall was so great that the earth shook and the ripple effect traveled like a 'tsunami', far and beyond touching the lives of all and sundry in the nations of the world.

The affluence, the surplus, the tower of Babel, everything that identified with riches vanished overnight. Cash flow stopped, aptly replaced by the deluge of the financial tsunami that encompassed all, rich and poor. From financial institutions to the man on the main street, everyone turned debtors overnight. The times became a classic case of debtors asking their debtors to repay. The sudden turn of events in the financial world made the small but hard-earned investment of Justin take a nosedive. His plan of working hard and be able to repay the bulk of his loans as soon as possible went 'kaput', and he ended up working harder to repay his loans.

In the times when the bubble was at its peak, Justin was not denied any loan by any of the financial institutions. Every loan enhancement application was positively entertained by the banks. There were credit bureaus to monitor the credit worthiness of clients but probably in that upward trend, the savvy money managers consigned the credit reports to the trash bins. Justin remembered that in India, loans were advanced by the banks for productive purposes only. Personal loans were far and few, always attracting a very high rate of interest as a deterrent. However, here banks were vying with each other to oblige the masses with lines of credit. They would come out with various terminologies to accommodate people while granting loans or increasing line of credit, encouraging people to refinance their houses to take that dream cruise to the Bahamas or the Caribbean. 'Take a loan, to pay the other loan' was the order of the day. The only criterion was the pay stub, the W2, form 1099 and the like.

Along with the bubble burst of 2008, the heavyweight financial institutions, the banks, and the hedge funds, which were on the top and affected the financial health of 'nations', tumbled down, in the process crushing the ordinary people who were otherwise clamoring to become the next millionaire. The financial tsunami vanquished the high and the mighty in a single day while the fate of the ordinary did not matter in the count.

Before the waves of the financial tsunami that invaded the system self-retracted, it was propagated that, to save the whole system from collapse, the big names among the fallen needed to be redeemed. The small or the proverbial 'Main Street' was left high and dry with an important piece of advice handed to them: undergo credit management sessions. The assets of none of the bigwigs were attached, whereas the dwelling places, the dream of the ordinary from the 'Main Street' went into foreclosure in hordes.

Jobs on Wall Street dried up, construction activity came to a grinding halt, and the big construction cranes that were standing on every nook and corner, now stood idle making whistling sounds due to the gusty December winds. In no time, even the hard-working people were forced to apply for unemployment benefits. Initially, many were hesitant to approach the social centers, but gradually, the need to pay utility bills and put food on the table for their children surpassed all inhibitions.

Justin waited for hours at a stretch in his car to get a job from his company. The crackling of the company radio in the car became such a rarity. Before the financial tsunami hit the city of Manhattan, Justin would see the yellow cabs and the black limousines, of which he was a part, racing feverishly across the city. Together, they would come to a screeching halt at the next red light, with their engines revving feverishly, so that the vehicles may zoom forward at the turn of green. There was work, more work and work for everyone.

Now, with the winter fast approaching and fall taking its leave, the bitter cold winds blew stronger. Justin, sitting in his car while waiting hours on end for a job, witnessed the fallen leaves being blown raucously across the road; the only difference being, the leaves did not stop at the red light and the NYPD cars with their sirens wailing did not ticket them.

'Vanity of vanities', says the Preacher; 'Vanity of vanities, all is vanity.' (Ecclesiastes 1: 2)

King Solomon, the probable writer of the above saying, was considered to be the wisest of all. Still, he found his own life experiences to be vain as a whole. Ever wondered why Solomon found his life experience to be vain?

The scripture says:

'He that troubleth his own house shall inherit the wind'. (Proverbs 11: 29)

With so many wives and concubines, he definitely troubled not one, but hundreds in his household. Therefore, in spite of being the richest and the wisest man in the world, his experience of life was vain. Proverbs, written by him, are a great source of wisdom to the simple but Solomon wrote these proverbs after experimenting with all the *don'ts* found in the Word of God. His own words of wisdom penned in two different books of the Bible did not benefit his own life.

That day, sitting in his car, Justin contemplated upon his own life. He was approaching his sixties and found truth in the word 'vanity' as repeatedly emphasised by the wise king. Spiritually, Justin had become bankrupt, socially, he did not have four shoulders to carry him if ever the need arose, and financially, he was a pauper in this land of opportunities, a non-entity in this land of promise.

Earlier, he knew the Bible like the back of his hand, now he knew the roads of this city like the back of his hand. Earlier, he gently led people to spiritual destination, now he drove them to their physical destinations.

Somewhere, the book of life says,

'...Repent and do the first works, or else I will come to you quickly and remove your lamp stand from its place—unless you repent'.

By the path that he followed, Justin had placed his lamp stand under the bushel, his life was heading towards the dark alleys of obscurity.

FATE

WAS JUSTIN DESTINED to get where he had reached in life? Justin was addicted to reading newspaper from his teen years. He would go through the headlines at a glance, then run through the comics and daily horoscope section before getting back to reading the news in detail.

At the start of the year, he would go to the central market in Delhi and buy a compact yearly horoscope paperback guide for himself. Oh! How sometimes the contents in the guide that made exciting future predictions would elate him and at other times, he would become sober, after going through the contents that predicted gloom and doom. In comparison, he noticed that his sun sign Sagittarius was better than the other sun signs, and would often predict heaven on earth in form of good love life, unexpected windfall of money, opportunity to travel abroad and all the goodies that make a person happy. Near the Old Delhi Railway Station in the city of Delhi, there was a public library, which Justin visited occasionally and right in front of it, a horde of palm readers and tarot card readers used to set up their shop on the walkway. Modus operandi of each being unique. A few would have an array of tarot cards neatly laid out in front of a cage with a parrot inside it. While passing through that place, Justin always found such tarot card readers, surrounded by people seeking to have a glimpse into their future. On making a payment, the fortuneteller running the show would get the parrot out of the cage and lead it to the neatly stacked cards. The parrot would then pull out a card with its beak and go back into the cage. The fortuneteller would read the contents of the card to the person, giving him an insight into the 'supposed' future happenings of their life. Justin, who was young and impressionable at that age, always watched this street show with fascination but never ventured to inquire about his own future from a mystic. However, Justin religiously went through all the horoscope references found in the newspapers, magazines, and the likes, and never missed any such material that he could lay his hands on. Horoscopes, sometimes became the main topic of discussion in many circles that he moved in, be it the bank circle, the social circle, or any other gathering.

After the initial months of starting the church work in Delhi, Brother Eric introduced another co-preacher known as Pastor Bose. The main attribute of this man was that he had a very shrill voice, compared with that of Brother Eric who had a rather deep voice. Judging from the personality of Pastor Bose, all were very skeptical about any positive impact that he could have on them. However, to the surprise of the congregants, Pastor Bose, instead of continuing in the footsteps of Brother Eric and preach subjects of grace, took a different approach and boldly started preaching and teaching on the subject of sin and God's plan of salvation. As a result of the teaching by Pastor Bose, it soon dawned upon Justin that referring to future things, asking from tarot readers, fortunetellers, etc., was blasphemous and, thus, a sin. He had been regularly attending the Main Line church since his childhood but had never come across such facts. Now, since Justin knew what was right, he shunned to have such prognostic views about one's fate.

His Own Hypothesis

JUSTIN DEVELOPED HIS own understanding about 'fate'. Half the world believes in 'fate' and the other half just uses the expression with no particular reason. It is simply a way of saying things. Well, it is not *fate* which leads where one is in life; it is how one conducts oneself in life. His opinion was that the journey of 'fate' can be understood under two broad subheads.

One as per him was that generally people born under the same roof, to the same parents, would have similar nature—as such, siblings tend to have common characteristics. If researched under quantitative study, his thinking was that the same would also hold good for people born under similar circumstances of day or night. It can also be said, that to a great extent characteristics of a person are influenced by the place where they are born, that is, to say those who are born in a particular country/region would be influenced by the prevalent culture. They may share generalised or common characteristic because they shared similar circumstances of time, place or a particular culture.

The above similarities, as drawn out by Justin's own philosophy, end there for it can be seen that the life of siblings born to same parents and under similar circumstances can ultimately get poles apart in the final count of life. Why??? This is because the actions taken by each individual in their lives would have a direct bearing on their fate. For what you sow so shall you reap.

The Word of God has a set of principles. If one sows righteousness, one shall reap the fruit of righteousness, and if one sows unrighteousness, one shall reap the fruit of unrighteousness. In accordance with the above statement, is it then that the outcome of one's life is the direct reflection of his or her *works*? However, the Bible says in the book of Romans that one's salvation is not dependent on the works of hands, bringing forth another truth, which states that 'salvation' is by the 'grace of God'.

To understand 'works that would lead to one's fate', one

has to understand that 'a' man can hand over the members of his body in the hands of God to do the works of righteousness, and 'another' can hand over the members of his body to his own carnal desires to do the works of unrighteousness. 'This choice' of ours to hand over the members of our body during our lifetime, dictates to a great extent where we ultimately reach in life while in our bodily state. Therefore, 'fate', as it is casually spoken of, is largely the result of the works of our hands and makes us reach where we ultimately get in life. Of course, there are always examples of good people suffering throughout their lives and bad people enjoying all the fruits of life.

That day, sitting by himself Justin understood the practicality of his own avouchment about fate, 'was he fated to get where he got in life'. The veil was slowly lifting up and the morning star started to shine upon him. Contemplating upon his life, he got a clearer picture of what happened with him. Forsaking all that he had in India—God, church, family and all that was dear to him—he had taken the big step of coming to America with the intent of settling down in life with Sushmita. In the process, unwittingly, he aligned his life to the 'fate' that brought separation from God and great worldly loss to him from which now there was no reprieve. All through his good fortune, he carved out his 'present' misfortune by sowing the *seeds* of his *deeds*, and now had to reap the harvest in line with God's word that says, 'as you sow, so shall you reap'.

The collapse of the financial system and the great recession that had spread its tentacles in every sphere of life had closed all doors of progress for Justin and had left him debt-laden. As per the requirement of his job, he made numerous trips to New York airports while ferrying his clients, many of whom may have travelled across the continents to meet their dear ones. At such times, Justin would longingly look at the airplanes taking off to the skies always wondering, when would he travel back home to meet his people?

The grief of not being able to see Armaan, his younger son, was unbearable. Justin missed him the most and fondly remembered each moment they spent together. Often with a grieving heart, Justin would remember the possessive nature of Armaan concerning him. When still a toddler, Armaan would expect Justin to understand everything that he tried to communicate in his baby garble. Armaan would never leave his side even for a moment and now, he has not seen Armaan for so many years. His heart ached at the very thought that he was not around his son, at times when he may have needed him the most. At times when Armaan would have needed guidance, at times in his teen-life when someone was needed to cheer him up, at times when the doubts about life needed to be clarified by someone who could be trusted—at such times, Justin was not there for Armaan. He was not there to clap for the achievements; he was not there whenever Armaan would have turned around looking for him.

Justin used to realise that compared to his grief, what Armaan must have undergone was much worse. Owing to the fact that he was being raised in the absence of his father whom he loved dearly. Sometimes, Justin would take out a greeting card that Armaan sent him when he must have turned fifteen, wherein he wrote, 'Dad, please come back for my sake'. Justin never discussed the contents of the card with Armaan. What explanation could he have given; how could he have told him that his father at that age won't fit into any vocation to earn a livelihood, that others won't welcome him to come back to take over the church again. Going back, Justin would have jeopardised his very survival, which ultimately would not be a cause of happiness for anyone. He had chosen a path where in spite of missing out on life, he could not retrace his steps. Justin had written his fate, he had chosen his destiny.

TRAP DANCE

IT WAS A day in summer with temperatures soaring to the other side of the nineties when people in the city of New York are always so oomph about the sizzling day with just one thought in mind—to run to the beach in their most outrageously skimpy beachwear. The most common pleasantries exchanged between strangers in New York on such a summer day would be, 'what a beautiful day' or 'I love this weather'.

Justin, on the other hand, never liked summers. He had had his fill of summer in India where such hot weather runs through the better part of the year, from March to September. He remembered when he was young, and his mobility was limited to walking or riding a public transport bus, he would scan the landscape to find shades under awnings or trees on the side walk to protect his skin from being scorched by the blazing sun.

On this scorcher, Justin stood in front of the vending machine at Herald Square subway station of Manhattan to buy the metro card before boarding a train for Jackson Heights in Queens where he lived. These underground subway stations become steamy hot during the summers. The crowd, on this particular Herald Square subway station, was a mix of people attired in office suits who were now retiring from their offices and the shoppers in their 'casual' casuals carrying tote bags loaded with their dream merchandise, handpicked by them from the string of mega stores that line up at the street level.

Swiping his metro card at the turnstile and briskly walking towards the 'R' train platform, he heard the sound of tap-dancing coming from the nearby 'Busking spot' created by the New York City to promote Busker and Street Performers. Justin, drawn by the rhythmic sound, came upon a big crowd which was cheerfully watching the young performers from some local dance company, doing the tap dance. The energy generated by the performers was so captivating that Justin slowed his pace and ultimately stopped to watch the performers. Tap dancing on their heels and then alternating with taps from their toes, the performers created an awesome rhythm without any musical instrument. They would occasionally step on the rectangular wooden board to create a variant in the sound and back again on the floor. The acoustic effect as produced in these underground subway stations was amazing, even Justin who did not have a single dancing bone in his body, started to tap his feet to the rhythm.

However, his pleasure was short lived, for that very morning, he had read a verse from the bible, which said:

'....Does a trap spring unless something sets it off?' (Amos 3: 5)

With his mind jumping from 'tap' to 'trap', his tapping of the feet came to an abrupt halt. Standing amongst the cheering crowd, his heart again filled with remorse that took over the better of him. He squeezed shut his eyes to stop himself from drifting into this mental setup that otherwise haunted him all the time. How he always wished for an opportunity to go back in time and rectify his mistakes.

He saw the proverbial 'trap' of the Bible dancing for him. The trap that was set off by him and his own actions in the prime of his life had now ensnared him viciously. Dancing, indeed, it was because Justin, a man of God, was caught up in it. Dancing, because 'the trap' knew Justin, who got completely embroiled in a covetous relationship with one of the creations of God, would not be able to extricate himself before it was too late.

Justin's mind was always full of thoughts—thoughts that were not very pleasant, thoughts about his financial situation—which were a constant source of drain on his energy. For the past so many years, all he was doing was work, work and work. Still, he did not see any respite from his labor. Coupled with this was his grief that saddened his heart all the time of not being a good father to his sons, particularly to Armaan.

Justin always regretted the fact that neither he had any direct input in the life of his son during his teenage years nor he was at hand for him when he entered adulthood. Such thoughts always depressed him. *Life is a one-time affair* and Justin had squandered the opportunity to achieve anything worth mention. His heart always pained to remember that he did not carry out his responsibilities towards his younger son, whom he fathered and literally forsook at the tender age of twelve leaving him to lead his life with nothing but a single parent—his mother.

In almost a decade, Justin had not set eyes on his son Armaan. Justin observed that whenever he called Armaan over the phone, though he genuinely sounded very respectful, he lacked the element of enthusiasm. He noticed that Armaan never took the initiative to call him or even answer his emails. The saying is that love grows with distance, but in their case, protracted distance was killing the love.

The pent-up passions for Armaan were like volcanoes that spewed smoke every now and then waiting for the time when all the churning emotions inside Justin would get the better of him, explode, and make him go extinct. He had lost everything that he once valued. Spiritually, socially and financially, he was bankrupt. How he wished someone in future would inscribe on his tombstone one word—LOSER.

EARNED THE WAGES

JACKSON HEIGHTS IS a place in the borough of Queens that is monopolised by South Asians. The streets are lined-up with varied configuration of stores selling wares brought from the countries of India, Pakistan and Bangladesh. This is a place where people from all the three countries live with perfect harmony, though the statement does not hold water about the relationship between the countries that are situated in the Indian subcontinent.

The market has a fair sprinkle of jewelry stores. Window-shopping there, sometimes Justin would be amused by the jewelry displayed for married women. The size of many of the displayed jewelry pieces were so huge and heavy, that it would make one wonder what damsel can be strong enough to carry such weight upon her person with elegance.

The peculiar aroma of South Asian food serving Indian, Pakistani and Bangladeshi cuisines—the famous chicken curry, chicken tikka, and samosas—would tempt one to splurge. Not to be outdone were a few restaurants serving Chinese noodles the South Asian way.

Then there were small kiosks usually at the entrance of bigger stores, where the vendor would sell *Paan* made with Beatle leaf. This delicacy, unfortunately after being chewed repeatedly, would leave one's mouth painted red on the inside and would further prompt the savourer to quietly and stealthily spit out the residue on some street corner, a disgusting habit by all standards.

On a pleasant spring evening, when the place was bustling with shoppers of all kinds, Justin parked his car at the parking meter, bought *Bhel-Puri* from one of the Indian restaurants and sat inside his car to eat. While he was savouring the delicacy, he noticed a traffic cop holding a hand held scanner intently looking at various stickers on the windshield of his car. Justin did not pay much attention knowing that he had paid at the parking 'Muni' meter and displayed the receipt on the dashboard. After a few minutes into his activity of savouring the *Bhel-Puri*, Justin noticed that the cop was gone and there was a traffic ticket stuck to the wiper of his car. Bewildered, he jumped out of the car and looked at the description of the ticket that was made out for $35. For a few moments, he could not comprehend the ticket as he had paid the parking money at the meter but on scrutiny, he realised that the ticket was written for the registration of the car that had expired the night before. Justin dumped the *Bhel-Puri* in the nearest trash can and hastily drove for the nearest DMV office for the renewal of his car registration that day itself, as that would save him from the penalty. Thirty-five dollars would not have been such a big deal but who wants to be ticketed? In local language they say, 'parking tickets suck'.

Traffic cops with hand held scanners in New York City is swift and merciless justice meted out on the spot.

Many a times, the punishment for sin is not swift and 'man', the mortal being, feels that justice would not be served. God, in his merciful nature, delays the punishment giving a chance to the sinner to repent and be saved. Justin had been treading this path of lustful pursuance outside his marriage for years together. Had he received a proverbial ticket from God, he would have taken note of his sinful activity and its consequences. However, this was neither a lapse on the part of God nor did He change the principle given in His word that says,

'Wages of sin is death' (Romans 6: 23)

When Justin was working in the bank, his monthly wages got deposited in his savings account. Any amount of the salary that remained in the account with the bank earned interest.

Justin the preacher of the Word had constantly ignored these daily facts of life. He thought since he is able to preach the Word of God, God is okay with whatever he was doing in his life. As God's justice to him was not swift, he slowly overlooked the fact that whatever he was doing was sinful and thus would reap wages. In spite of having a deep knowledge of the Word, he ignored the fact that a delay in chastisement would come with an added tag of accumulated interest.

When Justin decided to come to America, he thought God was guiding him to this new opening. When the church in Oklahoma sponsored him, he became so presumptuous as to think that God was on his side and was making a way for him, all the while ignoring the fact that he had left 'Him' for the sake of Sushmita.

'...for what fellowship have righteousness and iniquity?' (2 Corinthians 6: 14)

God has no fellowship with iniquity and naturally neither with the doer of iniquity. For many days, the melody of the song 'God will make a way for me, God will make a way', was stuck in Justin's head. He would regularly read the Bible and pray fervently with thanksgiving.

'He that turneth away his ear from hearing the law, even his prayer is an abomination'. (Proverbs 28: 9)

Justin's thanksgiving and prayer were in fact an abomination to God that He not only utterly rejected, but also despised.

However, all those who want to follow the dictates of their own hearts always try to twist the Word of God to their own advantage. Justin, doing what he was doing, never agreed that,

that was what he was doing. Satan had blinded him so completely that he never thought that the *above* happenings in his life which he presumed were for his betterment, were not from God. In pursuit of his own desires, he started to willfully ignore the above biblical verses and many more that were in fact a warning to sinners like him.

'And even as they refused to have God in their knowledge, God gave them up unto a reprobate mind, to do those things which are not fitting'. (Romans1: 28)

The Word of God is unchanging; however, sometimes man understands it only when the harsher side of it comes to pass upon him.

Now after so many years in America, still being the best country in the world to pursue dreams, Justin found himself wanting in everything. Hit hard by the ongoing financial crises, left alone in this big world, not able to see his sons, not able to pursue his passion to preach the Word of God, and instead having to ferry people from one place to another, another verse from the Bible struck hard at Justin.

'He will surely wind thee round and round, and toss thee like a ball into a large country; there shalt thou die…'. (Isaiah 22: 18)

To his dismay, now he understood clearly that it was not he who planned and executed the strategies to come to America to fulfill his desires, but it was in fact God who brought him here to twist and toss him around like a ball in this large country.

Strong hands are required to twist a ball. Then, when this twisted ball is thrown with force, it would not fall and bounce according to the laws of physics but would have a very erratic path and weird bounce. That is exactly what was happening with Justin; the unpredictability of his life now confused and scared him all the time.

'There shalt thou die' did not literally happen with him but Justin saw himself die every day for everything. When on Sundays he would attend some church, his heart would bleed from inside for not being able to preach. Whenever and wherever he would see some young child, his heart would double up with pain at the thought of his younger son. Whenever he would be in need of support of some strong hands, he would miss his elder son. Did Justin have a spirit of 'whoredom'? As mentioned in the book of Hosea:

'I know Ephraim, and Israel is not hidden from me; for now, O Ephraim, you commit harlotry; Israel is defiled.' (Hosea 5: 3)

Ephraim, the younger son of Joseph, was blessed out of turn instead of Manasseh, the elder one. In a very similar fashion, God blessed Justin out of turn on many occasions during his lifetime. Whether in personal life, professional life, in the bank, or as a pastor in the church, God seemed to bless him out of turn in spite of many other deserving people. However, like Ephraim, Justin gave precedence to his lustful desires over his love for God. On many occasions, God cautioned him through his prophets, pastors, elders, even by his wife Pearl, but Justin would not pay heed to the advice of any and at last, declared to leave God, showing a clear preference for one of God's own creations—Sushmita—over the Creator Himself.

The scripture is clear about the one who indulges in adultery:

'...Lest you give your honor to others and yours years to the cruel one. Lest aliens be filled with your wealth, and your labors go to the house of a foreigner. And you mourn at last, when your flesh and your body are consumed, and say, how I have hated instruction, and my heart despised correction!' (Proverbs 5: 9–12)

Justin labored a lot; however, his creditors snatched up the fruits of his labor. It seemed as if he had sold himself into the hands of such, and now he was just working for them and did not have any rights on the fruits of his labor. He could imagine himself as if he was living in the days of Gideon, when out of fear of the Midianites; Gideon was threshing wheat hiding behind rocks. Justin's position was even worse; at least Gideon screened himself behind a rock, but here Justin did not have the cover to hid himself or his labor behind anything. Everything that he did went to the creditors with a handful of sustenance left for him. God has promised to make the righteous the 'head' and not the 'tail', Justin had lost that privilege and had become the 'tail'.

Woe to the Au Revoir of that September night, when he was at the Delhi airport departing to the so-called 'new' start in life. That Au Revoir would ultimately play havoc in the life of everyone related to Justin; that Au Revoir which promised so many dreams that day would in the end, shatter all the dreams of his life. Everything that came his way after that *Au Revoir*, admittance to America, getting an opening with the church in Oklahoma, his R1 visa, etc., made him think was the 'good' coming out of it. He thought that his Au Revoir was acceptable to God. Alas, only now, he realised that the Au Revoir was in fact a vehicle to all the misery, grief and pain in the life that was to follow. He could have said Au Revoir to his sinful life and instantly gained God's mercy and all the goodness with it, but he bid Au Revoir to God himself.

Now he woefully felt that he was getting wasted and his body being consumed by the harsh labor day in and day out. Sitting alone in his car, many a times he would let out a loud sigh of anguish and say to himself, 'How different it would have been had he chosen the path of righteousness?'

TSUNAMI

A TSUNAMI HAS THE potential of causing havoc to places far off from its source of origin, with its ripple effects carrying the devastation to unsuspecting destinations. It was reported that the tsunami of 2004 that originated in the west coast of Sumatra killed several people in Africa, as far as 8000 kilometers from its epicenter. The earthquake that started the tsunami in December of 2004 had the longest duration of faulting ever observed; it caused the entire planet to vibrate as much as 1 centimeter and triggered other earthquakes as far away as Alaska.

Sin, just like a tsunami, creates ripple effects that send tremors in the lives of the near and dear ones, and has the potential to cause damage to unrelated people as well. Devastating effects of sin can be felt much later in future.

Today Justin, as a father, could feel the pain of the parents whose children conduct their lives, doing things without parental approval. Many a times, Justin even wondered what mayhem Pearl's parents would have undergone when he married her in the seventies against their wishes. What turmoil Sushmita's mother must have undergone, when on her short visit to the city of Delhi, she observed the flirtatious relationship between Sushmita and Justin. At one time during her short stay, she even confronted both of them and warned against the ill effects their relationship would bear. While boarding a train to Bangalore, she pleaded to Justin, 'Pastor, what you are doing is not right and beware that something similar may befall you'. Today, the 'tsunami of sin' had struck Justin with all its severity. Today Justin felt how one feels when one is not able to enjoy the togetherness with children, as they have strayed from the path that neither coincides with the thinking of their parents nor aligns with the common precepts of society at large.

At his age, this was the biggest punishment meted out by life to Justin. He really loved God but who would believe him? His biggest passion was to preach the Word of God but who would share the pulpit with him? When he arrived at New York to start the work in conjunction with the parent church of Oklahoma, there were many small churches led by different Indian and Pakistani pastors but people used to flock to his church to hear him. Justin had such an anointing to expound the Word that not many could match but today, they all had their churches and the faithful congregants, whereas Justin longed to even strike a biblical conversation with someone. Those who knew him still called him 'pastor', a prefix that now made him feel uneasy.

A sinful man does not die once; death haunts him repeatedly.

Death in every phase of life becomes his closest ally.

The easiest thing would be to die a physical death once and for all, but that does not happen to a sinful soul.

Every day, the agony of Justin's soul increased to intolerable levels. Every moment of his life, he writhed with the torment of all that was lost. None of the joys if there were any could take away the thoughts of his sufferings. However, in spite of all this, he had a strong personality and none could ever fathom the pain and agony he underwent each day. Such grief would have forced any mortal to contemplate the extreme step of taking one's own life but he never entertained such thoughts. His clients always complemented him for the comfortable journey they experienced in his car.

Whenever he made long distance calls to his sons, he talked with them in a very cheerful manner, enquiring about their well-being and important things concerning their lives. He would advise them on matters that they would talk about, he would bless them, pray with them, always try to take care of their financial needs as and when required. Neither his sons nor he would broach the subject of separation for they had done their reality check and learned to live with it.

The scripture says,

> *'For these things I weep; my eye, my eye overflows with water; because the comforter, who should restore my life, is far from me. My children are desolate because the enemy prevailed.' (Lamentations 1: 16)*

Undergoing all these sufferings, Justin occasionally became fearfully concerned about his sons. Justin feared that if his children would have to bear the burden of his sins or that the genes that destroyed his life would create the same havoc in their lives. Fear for one's own children is scarier than fear itself. Such thoughts repeatedly brought him to his knees and made him repent.

CONSEQUENCES

J USTIN HAD BEEN praying fervently to gain respite from his sufferings, but there was none in sight. Will he continually be tormented all his life? Many a days he felt what Job writes in his book:

'And now my soul is poured out within me; days of affliction have taken hold upon me. In the night season my bones are pierced in me, and the pains that gnaw me take no rest ... My garment disfigured; it bindeth me about as the collar of my coat ... Thou art turned to be cruel to me; with the might of thy hand thou persecutes me'. (Job 30: 16, 17, 18, & 21)

Who could fathom Justin's plight? The only difference between Job and Justin was that God allowed calamity to befall Job for He wanted to prove Job's righteousness to Satan, whereas Justin was on the receiving end from God for what he did in his yore years and never cared to retrace his steps from the path of iniquity.

Apart from his relationships with Sushmita, he had all the good traits of a nurturing pastor to his congregation. Justin was known to be a thorough gentleman, but who needs a thousand bullets to kill when one can do the trick?

What did the biblical character Esau do for whom it is famous that in spite of diligently seeking to reverse his infamous deed, he did not get a chance to be blessed by his father? The deed? 'One morsel' of food. In comparison, Justin's deed was much worse. How long will Justin have to undergo this suffering?

During his times of turmoil, Justin came to understand something very important about the consequences of sin.

In the parable of the prodigal son, Jesus tells the story of a man who had two sons. One fine day, the younger son demanded of the father to give him his portion of the inheritance. The father did so and the son gathered his inheritance and went to a far off place. He squandered all that he had and because of his riotous living, he became a destitute. While impoverished, he realised that he could still go back to his father and seek forgiveness, and that is exactly what the prodigal son did. When he came back to his father, he said,

'Father, I have sinned against heaven and in your sight...'
(Luke 15: 18)

It dawned upon Justin that mostly sin is committed against two entities—one is God and the other is someone upon this earth.

Sin has its wages, in other words, 'consequences'. At the time of repentance, God forgives and can absolve the man of consequences from his side but the consequences of sin that are committed against someone upon this earth may still haunt. The father of the prodigal son removed the consequences and restored the place of the son in his household, but most of the times the consequences of sin committed against a person remain. Reason being that in spite of being remorseful, one may not have approached the person who was wronged; and secondly, even if one approached that person, he or she may not have forgiven from the heart due to the hurt, loss or other inexplicable human emotions. Justin could understand that though God had forgiven him for his sins, the earthly consequences remain for which he still needed to do restitution by undergoing similar suffering. In fact, as per the Old Testament, the restitution has to be five times.

THE THREE R'S THAT LEAD
TO THE FOURTH

A S A PREACHER, Justin knew that whoever comes to God with a *repentant* heart, acknowledges his or her sin, and believing in His son Jesus receives forgiveness. Thereafter, one does not have to seek forgiveness for those sins repeatedly for one has to believe in the merciful and forgiving nature of God and know for sure that the sins are forgiven, once and for all.

David suffered immensely for the sin of adultery. He suffered shame, his kingdom never regained its glorious time again, his sons rebelled and last but not the least as per the punishment pronounced, his wives were violated openly in the knowledge of himself and everyone else. Justin was thankful that God, in his mercy, had not made him out to be an exemplary case by pronouncing extreme punishments. People still had love for him. There were many who still trusted him and there were many, who still wanted to hear the Word of God from him. He was thankful that even that day, God filled him with revelation from His word. So what if he did not have a platform to share it! The Bible says, *'The thief comes only to steal and kill and destroy...'.* Satan did come to Justin to steal and kill but by God's mercy, he could not utterly destroy him, Satan could not take charge of his soul. Justin was still spiritually alive and actively striving to seek God's

Kingdom and His righteousness. These thoughts of mercy would fill Justin with such an abundance of remorse that he had never felt before. *Punishment can cause regret, but mercy gives birth to remorse, for one's actions.*

Justin's remorseful heart repeatedly made him travel back in time and reminisce over his iniquities that he committed against God's holiness.

Justin remembered vividly that it was one morning of July 2009 and, as per habit, he was carrying the bible with him in the car. In between jobs from his car company, he had ample time to read the Bible and contemplate upon it. That day sitting in the car near La Guardia airport in Queens, he was waiting to receive a job on his computer. The wait was exceptionally long and during that alone-time in his car away from every other thought, Justin started reading the Bible from the book of Ezekiel. It was then that he was filled with the love of God in a new way, not because his deeds had brought his life to ruination, not because he feared financial crises, not because he missed his sons, but the reason of repentance was God himself. He realised that until now he had never reciprocated God's love.

Justin felt as if his love for God was like that of Judas Iscariot who although being a disciple of Jesus Christ was always hand in glove with the evil forces that worked against Jesus. Was that too harsh a comparison? No, certainly not. In fact, that is the stark reality for people like Justin. Judas claimed that he loved Jesus, lived with him continuously for three and a half years, broke bread with him and then betrayed him for thirty silver coins! Wow!! We say how awful his deeds were, but forget that anyone who not only claims to love God and is also ministering for the extension of His kingdom but still betrays God for whatever reasons—personal or otherwise—falls in the category of Judas.

In the past, Justin had claimed many a times, like others:

'For I am persuaded that neither death nor life, nor angels

nor principalities nor powers, nor things present nor things to come, nor heights nor depth, nor any other created thing, shall be able to separate us from the love of God...'. (Romans 8: 38, 39)

That day, he realised that his claims for loving God were so hollow. A man who is living a life of iniquity, a man who is relentlessly pursuing his own carnal desires in blatant contravention of the Word of God, cannot make such claims, however, emphatic the declarations may be. He cried out to God simply because, until now, he did not love Him the way He had loved him. He realised that he was routinely offering Judas kiss every day, he was routinely grieving the Holy Spirit of God every day, he was routinely trampling the very blood of Jesus that was meant for his sanctification. This realisation brought Justin to a different level of repentance and he felt as if he was transported into the very presence of God and His holiness where he could fathom his own unworthiness.

That day, he realised that, without regret and remorse, *repentance by itself* could not result in redemption. The three R's, *Regret, Remorse* and *Repentance,* are so important to reach the fourth R: *Redemption.* Justin's eyes welled up repeatedly.

How the dust of the earth, that he was, could defy and rebel against God the creator?

How could he, while covered with his ugly deeds, reject the love of the one who was the most beautiful?

How could he delude himself for so long with the creations of the creator?

How could he fix his gaze elsewhere when the Rose of Sharon was always near him?

How could he keep seeking joy in the world when God's nearness itself could give joy unspeakable?

Umbilical Cord

JUSTIN FELT THAT in spite of the torment he suffered daily, he had until then, never really detached himself from the clutches of the velvety strings of his covetous and carnal desires. That day, for the first time in his life, he truly cut the umbilical cord with his covetous desires acknowledging and declaring to himself that all his actions were sinful. Without any reservations, he asked God to wash him thoroughly from his iniquities, and to purge him with His hyssop so that he may be cleansed. Justin cried out to God to make him whiter than snow. He asked Him to create a clean heart and to renew a steadfast spirit in him. Justin beseeched God to build up his walls and renew his mind so that no evil thoughts may beset him again. It is written that you shall be free if He sets you free. Yes, and that day was the first time Justin truly asked God to set him free.

With tears filled-up in his eyes, it was a day of triumph for Justin—triumph upon himself.

It was a day of release, release from the fetters he had created for himself.

He evacuated the camp of Satan and safely returned to the camp of His father.

No one feasted for him on this earth, but he could hear the rejoicing of the Angels in heaven.

FLEE

I T WAS THE month of November back in the sixties, when huddled with hundreds of participants, Justin, wearing shorts and a T-shirt in the name of a tracksuit, was standing in the open at Model Town New Delhi police grounds. While applying for jobs after completing his graduation, Justin had come across an advertisement of the Delhi Police detailing the selection process into the cadre of 'deputy superintendent of police'. His educational qualifications matched the requirements and now, after getting through the written exam, Justin was participating in the endurance test being taken under various categories, out of which this last one, the 100-meter sprint, needed to be completed in the prescribed time.

Standing out in the open, waiting for his turn, was proving to be a damper as he felt the warmth of his body gradually diminishing and the ensuing shivering due to the morning chill taking over. The shivers were compounded with his anxiety to perform in the 100-meter dash within the stipulated time.

Running was never Justin's forte. In the school-gym, followed as well in college, he often participated in weight training programs but somehow always shunned running or jogging of any kind. Today, this last category of the endurance test was the only hurdle between him and the Delhi Police posting. The successful completion of the 100-meter dash would ensure Justin a place in another set of advanced placement tests and thereafter to the training institute of the Delhi Police.

'Why would they have the 100-meter sprint in the end when the participants were exhausted?' Justin asked himself. He was praying that he may be able to make it in the stipulated time. The sprint finally took place and alas, it wasn't meant to be. His shying away from any type of running made him fall out of the selected batch of candidates. Justin was disheartened, as the selection would have meant a progressive career opportunity.

Life moved on and Justin got a job with a bank and then, after almost two decades, he quit his job to become a full-time pastor in a church. Justin heaved a sigh of relief thinking that the necessity to run would no more hinder the progress in his life in this vocation. Little did he know that a Pastor or a minister needs to always practice sprinting. The biggest reason for Justin's downfall as a minister was that he did not learn the art to flee.

Paul, the greatest contributor to the New Testament, advises his young disciple Timothy,

'Flee also youthful lusts…'. (2 Timothy 2: 22)

On that day of his redemption, after undergoing untold misery in life and still reeling from the aftermath of his actions that jeopardised his chances of regaining back his losses, Justin realised how important it was for a minister of the Word to practice the art to 'Flee'. Joseph fled when tempted by the wife of the Egyptian captain of the guards. This art of fleeing, learnt very early in life, kept Joseph in step with God at all times and he reached the pinnacle of his career, predestinated for him by God, to become the second most powerful man in the land of Egypt.

All those great characters from the Bible who did not learn to flee fell by the wayside and suffered the consequences. Samson, who was a judge of the Israelites for twenty years, fell because he never learnt to flee in the face of temptation. King David, instead of running away from the rooftop from where he watched

Bathsheba taking a bath, conspired to get his own 'kinsman', the husband of Bathsheba, killed on the battlefront. King Solomon never refused any proposals of marriage alliances that came his way; though, by law, he was prohibited to marry outside of his own tribe and have several wives. As a result, the wise king, who was a devoted man, turned away from God at prompting by his numerous wives who worshiped other gods.

In today's modern world, revered names of pastors and leaders of mega churches that did not learn the art to flee fell by the wayside. Great names in the political arenas who did not take to flight at the first sign of temptation have vanquished in hordes with their names blotted out from the annals of history. Illustrious careers of great generals and national heroes have come to an abrupt end to the astonishment of the world at large. Justin had also realised too late that the ability to run was such an integral part of Christian ministry.

Today, while walking with God with utmost sincerity, Justin knows that even though God has enabled him to overcome his old nature, a sinful thought can still strike. Today also, that makes him run repeatedly to take shelter in the name of the Lord. For a lustful thought to occur, it is not necessary that there be an inanimate object, even a billboard on the road can break down one's defenses. The click of heels can still conjure up lustful thoughts. Images on magazine covers or random opening of web pages have the potential of drowning even a saint in the sea of iniquity. Even looking at a person, dressed piously, has the potential of causing degrading thoughts. The mind does not get polluted in pubs or clubs only and demeaning thoughts are not limited to youthful age, they can strike with fatality even when one is engaged in the most sacred activity.

Today, at every step, the righteous get defeated by immorality, impurity, indecency, anger, selfishness, envy, drunkenness, revelries and the like and thus become puppets in the hands of sin. The righteous will be saved if they build up the ability to flee the scene.

Flee when...?

Flee, before immorality penetrates

Flee, before impurity defiles

Flee, before indecency infiltrates

Flee, before anger clouds judgment

Flee, before selfishness blinds

Flee, before envy engulfs

Flee, before drunkenness overpowers

Flee, before riotousness ingresses

FLEE, FLEE, FLEE...

FRIENDS

THE SCRIPTURE CLEARLY states:

'Confess your trespasses to one another, and pray for one another…'. (James 5: 16)

Another reason that contributed to the downfall of Justin was the lack of any spiritual friends. Justin was a very friendly and social person, one who took care of his congregants in all aspects of their lives; in fact, his church members had such confidence that they would share almost everything concerning their families with him. They always found him standing with them in the thick and thin of life, praying with them, counseling them. He would be the first to reach them in times of trouble. The congregants drew strength from Justin when life demanded more than they could endure. However, this also made him a man lonely at the top. What he lacked in his ministry was a friend who could give him some advice when needed. His personality deterred even his contemporaries from the leading sister churches to approach him concerning anything.

Today, he understands the importance of a spiritually strong friend, who would not hesitate to point a finger at his faults. The need to have a spiritual friend, particularly of the same sex, has great importance in one's ministry. Same sex, because the temptation to develop inordinate affection between them would be highly unlikely. A friend, who is spiritually mature, would be able to help in times of temptation and desist from indulging in gossip. This friend would be a support when one is standing on slippery grounds and would have no qualms about calling a spade a spade.

Today, Justin understood that a minister does become a star performer for his congregants, and it is human for the followers to give extra attention to charisma of the leader. However, this is the very time when the minister needs to be more vigilant about one's conduct. The friend should have a free reign to point out circumstances where one would go wrong. The minister should be able to share/confess with this friend one's weak feelings with regard to the opposite sex that can develop from time to time. It is not only the feelings of inordinate affection, it can be strong envy, it can be strong dislike, it may be an unhealthy competition with another minister that may overpower a minister from time to time. It may be the temptation to go the unrighteous path when a financial crisis looms large. It may be a plain unbelief in God Himself, which Satan brings upon unsuspecting ministers on different occasions. In all such and many more pitfalls on the way that one may encounter, the friend would come to the rescue; to caution, to deter, to make see sense, to pick up the fallen comrade without rebuke, and last but not the least, to pray with such minister in the times of trials, temptations and tribulation.

The scripture says,

'When the enemy comes in, like a flood the Spirit of the Lord will lift up a standard against …'. (Isaiah 59: 19)

'Such a friend' could have saved Justin in his ministry, for all those who come with conviction to serve the Lord, truly want to glorify His name through their lives, but to be successful one needs to ensure that the basic guard is not let down. That is why a conglomeration of churches is better than a single mega church or a single famous preacher running the show. For it would not be very long before that the minister sitting alone at the top would be alienated, and Satan would find umpteen opportunities to pounce upon the unsuspecting mortal, who had unknowingly and unwittingly learnt to bask in glory; the fall will not be far.

ALAS

Bible says, 'Some men's sins are clearly evident, preceding them to judgment, but those of some men follow later.' (1 Timothy 5: 24)

SOONER THAN LATER, the judgment of sin is such a reality. Sin follows a person right after and after a certain time it overtakes; it is then that the dreadful weapon of sin 'the consequence' would mercilessly tread the sinner under its feet.

It will be glorious if none, particularly people who are serving God, may fall to temptations and thereafter suffer 'the consequences', which to the unsuspecting doer can be beyond human endurance. At the first sign of sorrow on the face of the loved ones, the first sign of welling of their eyes, the first time a well-wisher comes and reprimand; take note and repent, for thereafter sin will ensnare in such a powerful way that escape won't be easy. Ignoring the above puts, the person on a protracted walk on the path of unrighteousness that would completely blind and *present* no opportunity to make amends.

Justin ultimately gained some semblance of normalcy to his life, but the ground that he had lost simply could not be recovered. The bygone teenage years of his sons could never again experience his fatherly love. Recovery of life after the tsunami of sin is such an arduous task. Resources may be there to cope up with the demands to rebuild, but each time one is upon the ruins, the pain would return; each time one is reminded of a life wasted by one's actions, the remorse would come back. Do not give in to a life time of tears; today is the day to repent, today is the day of salvation.

Somewhere the Bible mentions, 'The days of this life that are seventy years, and if by reason of strength they are eighty years', but then not only the length of one's life the happiness of it is also so very important. It is the question of a whole lifetime, which is too precious and too long to be ignored and sacrificed. Generally speaking, everyone values life, but at times there are those who are devoid of any understanding and do not learn even by others' experiences; they have destined their lives for the slaughter. Fortunate are those who learn early and escape the aftermath of sin; the tumultuous waves of tsunami would not overwhelm them; they are the one who can run and take shelter in the name of the Lord that is the strong tower and be saved.

www.ingramcontent.com/pod-product-compliance
Lightning Source LLC
Chambersburg PA
CBHW050937120626
46552CB00001B/253